The Idealists

Sara Purdon

To the people that never gave up on me

And to the people that helped me make this book possible

PROLOGUE

Winnifred

Summer, 1953 was when my whole life changed, the night of May 21st 1953, school had just ended and my parents were out of town, on a casual date night. while my oldest sister Trixie was at college studying nursing at Fordham and was ought to come home in a few days, my other sister Evelyn was home with me. She was doing her normal causal thing. She would sit alone wait for one of our friends to call us. And me, I would read a book, Whether it's Jane Austen or The Bronte Sisters. No in between.

We heard crashes and sirens that night Little did we know that it would change everything. Forever

As we got that call, Evelyn was the one to pick it up. Her face went from excited, to shocked and concerned at the same time.

"Winnie! We have to go!" She said anxiously.

"What?"

"Just we have to."

"Why?"

"Mom and dad..." she knew she had to be strong, "Mom and dad were in an accident and we have to go."

"Oh my gosh!" I was definitely on the verge of tears.

As we rushed to the hospital, we ran over and saw trixie. She rushed over to Evelyn and hugged her tightly. She saw me in pain and hugged me even harder than she did Evelyn.

"You okay Winnie?"

I was already in tears.

"Is everything okay?"

Trixie shrugged, she had only just gotten the call. But didn't know anything. Trixie was probably thinking what could happen if things went horribly wrong. Would all her plans and dreams change? She didn't know that everything would.

As the doctor came in and with the expression on his face. She knew... she knew that everything would be different.

CHAPTER ONE

<u>Winnifred</u>

August 1953

Since the death of our parents, things started to be completely different between me and my sisters, Trixie, my oldest sister who I considered myself to be close with, we can never get more than 3 syllables from each other, she had to drop out of her dream college to raise me and Evelyn, which is probably one of the reasons she is always so upset. Or maybe it was the pressure of being a twenty-one-year-old college dropout looking after a fourteen-year-old and a sixteen-year-old, or maybe it is the fear that social workers will separate us if we don't behave, even though it is very hard to not get into trouble in New York.

I do often feel like Trixie takes her aggression out on me. Is it because she knows I can take it or the fact that she knows I can fight back?

Evelyn is handling everything better than all of us put together. Which is something she doesn't do often. She is always been the type to get emotional or be sensitive during these types of situations. I think it is because she knows she has to be strong. Not only for me but for Trixie. Along with that, she had to deal with the fact that her boyfriend, Brian Scott over a year had been two-timing her for months. Brian is a rich kid, he is the mayor's son someone I could never really tolerate. And the girl he cheated on her with, is another rich girl, her name is Abigail Jackson, she is rich because her father owns a car dealership or something. I never understood why anyone would want to hurt Evelyn, she is probably the kindest, sweetest girl anyone will meet. Her only downfall is that she is quite naive. But overall, she is a great sister and a good friend to the rest of us.

I always considered myself to be quite independent. Maybe it was a part of me wanting to grow up fast and realizing that I had to grow up fast. I knew that I wasn't alone. I had a lot of people beside me. I had my friends and my sisters.

August was the month where we had to get everything on track. I was about to start my freshman year of high school, however, I was taking some sophomore courses. Trixie was a little bit more stressed than normal since it was the fact that she was getting more shifts than normal. As I walked down the steps and greeted her, her hazel eyes looked super baggy due to the lack of sleep she was getting. Her shirt was filthy, and she looked like she hadn't showered in days. She took at the envelopes from yesterday's mail looking distressed but also relieved since they weren't bills that weren't overdue and needed to be paid.

A part of me really missed the old Trixie, the Trixie before mom and dad died. She was a great sister and was always out looking after us, she was kind and never scolded at us, some of the times she would, but wouldn't that be normal for sisters to do that. Trixie was seven years older than me so it was hard for both of us to stay close. By the time she started High School I started second grade, there were times where I would want to hang out with her and her friends, but she never let me. I didn't understand then, but I do now.

"Good Morning Trix." I said walking downstairs.

While Trixie was getting ready for the day, Evelyn was sitting there waiting for me. Evelyn always was someone I admired growing, she was kind and beautiful, and had all the boys wanting to be with her. She had porcelain skin, with dark brown hair and blue eyes as bright as moms were, so who wouldn't blame them, she looked like a real-life Cartoon Character. She may be older than me, but she is more innocent and naive than I have ever known. Even more innocent and naive than my friend Jenny. But that morning, Evelyn didn't have her normal smile this that was the day she found out about Brian cheating on her. She looked like Juliet after she found Romeo dead from the poison.

"Do you wanna talk about it?" I asked her.

"No, not really" She sighed.

Moments passed and the doorbell rang, I decided to go get it since I knew who it was. I open it to see Valerie Darling, a girl who I will admit when I first met her I was absolutely terrified of her, since she was in a gang in Texas. Val is someone that people look at and they are terrified of her. She has a cold mean look to her, and was tall for a girl around 5'7" maybe 5'8", she also had dark brown hair and dark brown eyes, with a dark tan. Val also had a lower-toned voice for a girl and wore dark colors all the time, and had a thing for leather jackets. Valerie, like me is being raised by her older sibling, her mom died a few years ago and her father was put in prison. She is currently being raised by her brother Max. He is a year older than Trixie and they actually went to High School together. Max is tougher than nails, he is someone that can easily come to defend you in battles, I wonder where Valerie gets the toughness from.

"Hey Winnie," she said barging in, taking a piece of bacon, "What's the plan for tonight?"

I shrugged "Bonfire?"

"Alright, it's a plan."

As Valerie took another piece of bacon, my other best friend, Jenny came in, she was someone completely different from me and Valerie combined. She was more timid and vulnerable, with a really kind heart, I definitely saw her as a girl that was hurt too many times. Her fragile and petite physique did not help her state, she was really small for a fifteen, only, 5'2" almost sixteen-year-old girl. She had blonde hair, with doe blue eyes, and was shorter than anyone. Valerie walked over to her as soon as she walked in.

"Jenny, how is it going?" Val asked

"I'm just ready to go to school," Jenny said silently. Her voice was almost as soft as Evelyn's. I could tell she just wanted the day to be over with. Myself, Jenny, and Valerie immediately left, we completely forgot about saying goodbye to Trixie. I was just hoping that things would be different today. Today with my sister and I getting along, hopefully the Richies won't be going after us constantly. Which I knew couldn't be possible. It was never going to be possible.

CHAPTER TWO

Evelyn

I never thought he would cheat, Brian Scott, the golden boy of our school to cheat. And why me? Like I try so hard to make sure things work out and they never work out for me. Where do I go wrong? It's like I just want to prove to the world that I am a good person. Yet, things come to bite me in the ass. Will I ever get my happy ending? Will I ever find the person I am supposed to be with? That's all I ever wanted.

As Winnie, Jenny and Val went to the bonfire. Trixie came into my room with my best friend Jo. Jo is the spunky, outgoing aggressive girl that everyone needs in their life. She always wore Jeans and Flannel most of the time. and always had her hair up in a bun. Jo was always the type of girl that was not afraid to put up a fight. She was someone I never knew I needed. Along with that, she was of average height with a curvy figure with brown hair and brown eyes, and just never cared what people thought of her, which was something I have always admired about her. Another one of my friends, Paulette Andrews, was very similar to Jo, she had a goofy personality to her that we loved. With her outgoing energy, you could never tell if she was drunk or not, She would be drunk off of life.

Paulette and Jo came into my room, I was sitting alone depressed. Jo came to sit next to me, and she just decided to pull me out of bed. Paulette brought me over food. Fries and a nice vanilla milkshake. My favorite.

"Feeling better Ev?" Paulette asked me, clearly concerned and serious.

"No. Not really?"

Jo took my hand to lighten up the mood. I was on the verge of tears. I never thought this would happen. Brian and I were together for a goddamn year. People said it wouldn't last. Maybe he didn't like that I wasn't interested in putting out yet.

"if I see him," Jo stated, "He will end up severely injured."

"Please don't" I replied a little more calmly. I knew how much Jo always wanted to protect me it is something I have always admired about her. But she can't fight my battles all the time for me. As much as she loves to do it for me, I wish to fight my own battles from time to time.

"Jo?" Paulette asked, "Can we skip violence for one day?"

Jo nodded. For once Jo chose not to fight someone for me. Sometimes I wish to be in charge of my own battles and lead for once. But it can be difficult since I have lived in fear my whole life, I feared people, failure and most importantly being alone. But I knew I would never be alone. I had me beside me no matter what had occurred, it seemed like everyone always wanted to protect me.

Hours have passed, and me, Paulette and Jo were hanging together and we heard the door knock.

"I'll get it," I said, as I walked over to the door, I opened it to see him. Dean. Dean Richards. He is Abigail's ex-boyfriend who has been in jail all summer for an armed robbery or something. He is your everyday stereotypical trouble maker. He wore leather jackets all year long. He had jet black hair and green eyes, he was quite tall about 6'2" with broad shoulders and a really nice physique. He just knew how to charm a girl in a heartbeat without even trying. But he was one of the types of guys that would flirt with someone, sleep with her and then go about with their day. Something I was not about.

"Afternoon Dean," I said confused.

"Evelyn." He said with his husky voice.

I sighed, I was slightly confused on why Dean Richards was at my house. Is he trying to run away from cops? Or did he want me to get back at Abi? I had to know what I was getting myself into. Especially with Dean at my door.

"Who's at the door?" Paulette asked.

Jo and Paulette walked over to the door, and saw Dean. Jo gave him a dirty look immediately. I knew this wasn't going to be good.

"What's he doing here?" Jo asked

"I'm wondering the same thing." I said.

"Dean Richards at our door..." Paulette said, "This can only mean one thing, you guys. Dean is horny."

Jo then slapped Paulette's hand, and i looked straight at Jo. She was getting protective again. But I had to assure her that this could be okay.

"Alright, you wanna know why I'm here?" Dean asked.

I nodded. I knew he had something up his sleeve for us. Either he wanted to screw me or screw with me. This couldn't be good.

"Alright, may I come in?" Dean asked

I nodded. As He came inside, the first thing he did was take off his jacket leaving him in his boots, wife-beater shirt, and jeans. I couldn't help but stare at his broad shoulders. Something about them, something about him in general. I know I am told things about him, and how he is seen as the town's asshole, the type of guy that is not afraid to make kids cry, and take his frustrations out on the whole world. But he is also not afraid to punch a guy or two if they were in his way.

"So, Dean..." I sighed. "What is it?"

"Can you come by the Rebel Pony tomorrow night?" He asked.

I was so shocked. What did he want to do with me?

"I'm sorry, but why..." I tried asking what was going on.

"Do you wanna seduce her?" Jo interrupted me. She was ready to fight him if she had to she has disliked Dean for the longest time, knowing his past and everything he does around here.

"You wish Evelyn." After the comment was made, Jo rolled her eyes. She knew he was going to bring trouble. But I needed to know why he wanted me to see him.

"What is going to happen?" I asked.

"I had a few ideas." Dean sighed, coming to sit next to me, "I was thinking of telling them people hooked up, but nobody would buy that. No Offense "Little Miss Virgin" But then there's me, who can have any girl I want. So can we shake?"

I was very hesitant with negotiating with Dean. Knowing how he is, I was honestly scared of getting hurt in the process. Dean is definitely someone we consider to be a heartbreaker.

"Do you trust me kid?" He asked,

I nodded. But he noticed how nervous and reluctant I was about this. Because Dean is just someone I didn't know if I can trust. But he looked like he seemed upset about Abi two-timing him. And came by to sort of check to see if I was alright, maybe I think. I don't know anymore.

I truly believe with all the thing said about Dean Richards, he is someone deep down with a good heart, regardless of what anyone says. However, he is someone that can snap in a heartbeat.

"Jo. Paulette. Can you two leave?" I asked. They both listened. And Jo left giving him the finger. The room was silent for a couple of minutes. Dean looked at me for a few seconds.

"Whats going to come out of this?" I asked.

"Honestly. I have no idea."

CHAPTER THREE

Trixie

Things were getting tougher out here, it was like I can't eat or sleep around here. All I am doing is working, cleaning, making sure the girls are okay because right now it seems like that is the only thing that matters. Making sure my younger sisters were safe. But no one really seems to notice how hard I am working to make sure that they are safe and happy.

I wanted to take Evelyn and her friends to the diner to help Evelyn get her mind off her breakup. They were together for over a year and he had the audacity to cheat on her. With another richie who was in a relationship... IS HE SERIOUS?

As we reached the diner, Evelyn and her friend Jo sat down in a booth and I decided to sit with them. Paulette, who arrived a little later met up with us 10 minutes later. Paulette's face was lighted up with energy... yet when is it not? and it is something all of us can really need in the worst times. She helped me the first month after our parents died, whether it was cleaning, doing laundry, or just anything that would help me. Which were something and someone I really needed since I felt like I had to go through everything alone. The diner was the perfect distraction. I was able to forget about everything. Just spending time with my sister and her friends, some may find it weird that I am hanging out with my younger sister's friends but it is something I needed to do. Just to treat her to dinner.

As the food came around, we started to chat about the events that have occurred, from Dean, the town troublemaker being out of jail after an armed robbery at a bank with his troubled friends, and the fact that his girlfriend cheated on him while he was in jail, with Evelyn's boyfriend. Which was something I was very annoyed about since Brian was not my favorite person and he was finally started to earn my respect.

"Feeling better Ev?" Jo asked her, I look at Jo and she seemed concerned more than her usual crazy and cocky persona. Evelyn shook her head, I could just tell in her eyes that she was not happy.

"You don't have to talk about it," I said to her as she looked down at the floor. Evelyn barely said a word the whole time we were there. Especially when the food was here and when Jo and Paulette were finding ways to be funny and goof off and cheer her up. Paulette even tried to cheer her up, she started by blowing bubbles in her milkshake, that still did not work.

"Don't worry about it. Brian is an asshole." Jo claimed.

"He is." Paulette agreed, "he has some nerve to cheat on you."

A little after going to the diner, and after Dean came by, I went home as Evelyn, Jo and Paulette decided to wait for Winnie, Jenny and Valerie. I walked home constantly thinking. Thinking about how I was going to support my sisters and how I was going to pay the bills. My parents were dead. I don't know if my grandparents are even alive, so I can't even reach out to them. Valerie's brother, Max is my age and is in the same situation. The only difference is that his father was in jail, in the middle of nowhere Texas.

All I am trying to do is be the best guardian I can possibly be, I want my sisters to have a spectacular future. Winnifred can do it, with her grades and hard work, she can probably get to any college she wants. She can also get a full-ride if she could, to literally any school. And I know how difficult this is for Evelyn and she is trying to keep it together and be strong for me and Winnie. Being the sweetheart that she is, she never gets involved in our arguments and always is making sure that I am okay in every situation. Knowing that I constantly am fighting with Winnie, who is only fourteen, it seems really ridiculous that I am constantly arguing with my fourteen-year-old sister, but sometimes she thinks she's twenty-one and can do whatever she wants.

The night ended and Winnie and Evelyn came home. It was a little later than I would have wanted them home. I was already annoyed enough with frustration, and I thought the best idea was to take it out on Winnie.

"You're late," I said.

"I know, that was my fault." Evelyn stated, "I was talking to Valerie and we lost track of time."

"You know you have a curfew, use it," I said.

"It's fine Mom... I mean Trixie" Winnie responded in a snotty teenager tone.

"We have rules in this house and I would recommend you follow them! Seriously!"

"Well Sorry..." Winnie snarled, "I am fourteen I will be fine!"

Winnie walked away and rolled her eyes. Evelyn followed her and made sure she was alright. But Evelyn was always the peacemaker in our arguments. It wasn't right for her to be caught in the middle of it all.

But we both need to control our tempers. Especially myself.

I sighed.

Things were no longer going to be easy.

Things were never going to be easy again.

And only with time, things are going to get even more difficult, which was something I needed to prepare myself for.

CHAPTER FOUR

Winnifred

I never thought people would attend the bonfire. I didn't expect to see this happening. I was starting high school. But with the rivalry with the Richies getting tenser, it would all be difficult. I saw some of Abigail's friends in front of me. I also saw Valerie terrorizing 10-year-old kids which was normal behavior for her, she always hated children and loved making them cry scaring them until they were out of their seats. I heard a loud scream from behind me knowing it was Val. She was loud and had no problem scaring kids. I look over my shoulder and knew it was her. Maybe it was the sound of two children crying, I looked over at her in disappointed and just asked why.

"I hate kids." She shrugged.

I laughed at her, which I felt bad for. But knowing Valerie, I knew that she just loved to make people cry.

Scaring kids were one of the reasons I found myself scared of her, but Jenny was never scared of her, she had other things to be scared of than Valerie Darling.I look the other way and see Jenny eating a s'more. She looked the happiest she has been in a long time, who would've known that a s'more would make a difference in a sixteen-year-old girl's life, Jenny's life was tough. She had parents, but they were not as loving. Her father was abusive and her mother was equally psychotic, she was an alcoholic, her father had an affair a while back and Jenny caught him and she told her mother immediately. Ever since her relationship with her parents was horrid, so she decided to stay away from them as possible. My parents knew about Jenny's situation and let her stay over whenever she can and made sure she was warm and well-fed until the word of adoption was in order for her, but we couldn't due to financial reasons. Which I felt horrible about since Jenny is the sweetest person I know.

"You in heaven Jen?" I asked as she smiled, her eyes lit up like a little kid in a candy store. I smiled for her as well. "I'm glad, you look happy," I mumbled.

Valerie tapped on my shoulder a little after, she clearly just was bored and wanted to leave. She looked over to see a hungry Jenny.

And I saw the Richies afterward, I didn't want to be near them one bit. The only one I tolerated was Julia Rose, she was tall and pretty, she had light brown hair and light brown eyes. We went to middle school together and we were in a few classes together even though she was a year older than me, she was smart and kind and was always looking after me when I moved to New York. She waved to me and I waved to her back. Valerie saw her wave to me and was immediately annoyed and just was ready to leave. We followed her orders as she push me and Jenny away from the food.

A few minutes have passed and we are walking in the dark New York. As we were talking and laughing, we heard a sound of a car pulling up in front of us.

Oh no!

I recognized that Red convertible anywhere. The car pulled up and I recognized all them. Julia was in the back seat along with blonde and bubbly Sandra White, and in the front was Abigail driving and in the passenger seat, aggressive and blunt Barbara Keller.

"Where are you girls going?" Barbara asked as Abigail kept driving and we kept walking "Hello? Can you speak?"

"Hey Back off!" I shouted. Later Valerie flipped the bird over to Abi which ended up instigating things a little more.

"Hey, Whore!" Valerie shouted. "Why don't you go fuck yourself!?"

That only added fuel to the fire.

"Stop the car Abi!" Barbara shouted. Abi followed her orders and stopped the car, Barbara went out of the car and Abi followed her. We were not worried about what was going to happen because we knew Valerie could take them down. But I saw the fear in Jenny's eyes, worried that things were going to be bad, with Val's strength, we would have nothing to worry about.

"Guys let's not do this," Julia stated as Sandra got out of the car, not listening to what Julia had to say, "You know how I feel about fights."

"What is your problem?" Abi shouted at Valerie, going close to her, Abigail asked her one of the stupidest questions she could ask.

"Maybe it's the fact that you slept with Brian." I stated, "My sister's boyfriend."

"Oh that little cry-baby prude," Sandra stated.

"You realize that she didn't give him what he wanted? So I did." Abi shouted.

"You are such a whore." Valerie shouted.

I looked to see Jenny tensed up. She sat down and covered her ears to forget about the fighting I wanted to rush over to her but Barbara was all up in my face.

"get out of my face!" I shouted.

As the fighting continued, with Julia coming by to try and break it up, and with Jenny scared out of her mind. And Barbara and Valerie going head to head, and also taking on Abigail, it seems like things were never going to end. All of us were so upset, and Abigail's friends justified her cheating and were talking poorly about Evelyn, who would never hurt a fly, they should just respect her and her boundaries and who she wants to be with. I didn't think that the fight would be broken up, by a guy named Dean... Dean Richards. The Dean... The Troublemaker of town.

"Ladies. Ladies. What is going on here?" his husky voice said walking over.

"Hi Dean..." Jenny said a little bit more calm than normal.

"What are you doing here?" Abi asked him in a snotty tone, hoping for him to get away. But he wasn't going to leave. He was going to help us, turns out the town criminal had our backs.

"Well, It seems like things look a little off... with Abigail here," Dean stated with a little smirk. "And I just wanted to see if you needed any... assistance."

"Were fine." snarled Barbara, who rolled her eyes at cocky Dean.

"We don't need your assistance Dean..." Abigail stated.

"Listen to Dean, Abi." Julia said to her.

"Just helping three lovely ladies," Dean smirked.

"Is lovely the correct term for me Dean?" Val stated as Dean and I gave her a dirty look, Val always tends to say the snarkiest, most sarcastic things at the worst times possible. She also gave dirty looks to the Richies who were immediately stunned by Valerie's attitude. As Sandra and Julia walked back into Abi's car, Abi shoved Dean and stormed off while Barbara rolled her eyes.

The night ended and I went home with Evelyn. I knew it was past curfew and I knew that Trixie wouldn't be too happy. As we reached the front door, Trixie was outside waiting for us, she was not a happy camper to see that we were late. I looked straight at Evelyn, who later looked straight at me. We knew she was strict and was not going to be happy with us.

"You're late," Trixie shouted

"I know, that was my fault." Evelyn stated, "I was talking to Valerie and we lost track of time."

"You know you have a curfew, use it," Trixie snapped.

"It's fine Mom... I mean Trixie" I responded in a snotty teenager tone.

"We have rules in this house and I would recommend you follow them! Seriously!"

"Well Sorry..." I snarled, "I am fourteen I will be fine!"

I walked away rolling my eyes, Evelyn followed me. As we got inside, Evelyn grabbed my hand. She looked almost upset with me for talking back to Trixie, knowing that I am not afraid to put up a fight when it comes to standing up to myself. Evelyn on the other hand knew that Trixie had enough on her plate and did not want to bother.

The night went by and it was time for us to go to bed. Evelyn was ready for sleep. I spent most of the night thinking. Thinking about whether or not Evelyn and I would be sent to a girl's home. Whether or not Trixie would be able to handle me. Or even Evelyn.

"Ev?" I asked softly

"Hm?" She responded

"What would happen if social services don't approve of our lifestyle?" I asked her. She got up and walked over to the bed where I was. She looked at me and knew I was being serious. With all the questions and all of the concerns I had. Towards me, her and Trixie. We had lives in New York, we had friends that loved us so much and the whole town that cared about us.

"Well, we can be sent away..." she stated, "Possibly separate from one another, it depends on the situation." She explained how if I did something, I can be sent to a stricter girl's home and the same thing with Evelyn. Evelyn is not the type to do anything that would cause harm to anyone. She was smarter than that to not start anything. Whether it was a fight with the Richies. Or if it was an argument with Trixie, she doesn't try to run away from home, which I already have tried to do twice. I never went anywhere when I left. I just hid at Valerie's for a few hours and Trixie found me. Anyway. Evelyn was smart, Evelyn was sweet, and never fought. She just kept quiet in situations.

"Like hell, they'll send me to a girl's home!" I said, "Trixie just wants me gone doesn't she?"

"She has a lot of responsibilities Winnie." She replied, "She is frustrated and she has a lot going on."

I knew that Evelyn reminded me so much of mom. She was kind and had the soft, gentle voice that she had, same copper brown hair, fair skin, and crystal blue eyes. She was always mom and dad's favorite, it was clear for all 16 years of her miserable life, she had some health problems as a child from ages six to eight but all of those got taken care of.

Me on the other hand, I was always told I had a gift. I was smart, or I was told I was smart. I was ahead of most of the kids in my grade, I am a freshman taking sophomore math and English. I just did not understand why people in my family did not see how I was trying to be the best version of me and didn't see how nobody saw me for who I was rather than me being the youngest. Because I am Winnifred Grace Martin damn it.

"I just want things to be normal just as much as you do. But things will never never be normal." Evelyn said quietly, "Now get some rest, first day of school tomorrow."

Trixie came in as soon as Evelyn went, checked in on both of us. She smiled and did not know that I was awake and saw her smiling at me.

"Good night girls." I heard her whisper as she closed the door.

I really needed to know when she was in a good or bad mood, the days she will like me and days she won't, I really needed to keep my eye out on the days she hates me. But things were getting more and more frustrating by the day.

CHAPTER FIVE

Evelyn

The day after the bonfire, I woke up earlier than usual. I have no idea why, maybe it was because I had a hard time sleeping with the fear I had all night, fear of how people were going to perceive what happened between me and Brian. I knew people would talk about it, they would say that it was my fault. I was the problem. I didn't put out, I didn't satisfy his needs. But Abigail, she did, she satisfied him. She gave him what he wanted.

I went downstairs and saw a jammed-up Trixie cooking breakfast, and Winnie reading a book, probably the same books she usually reads. Whether it was Jane Austen or the Bronte Sisters, it was nothing new in the

Martin family household. Our typical morning was Stress, a quick breakfast, and later arguing over running late to work and school.

The morning went by and I rushed over to school with Winnie. Trixie did not even bother to say goodbye, a part of me did not want to bother her since she had to rush over to work. Jo was waiting for us outside along with Paulette. Paulette had more energy than normal, she didn't have any alcohol, which is the way she usually would start her morning. And Jo was a lot calmer than her loud, cocky self. All of us were together in a group, smiling, but a little bit of fear was with me as everyone was set for school.

As we got to school, Jenny and Valerie were right behind us and Winnifred left us to go hang out with them. Jo and I went into the school only to be blocked by Abigail's minions. I knew we could take them. Since they were a lot weaker than we were. As we walked right passed them, Barbara, one of Abi's friends continued to follow us.

"Whats the matter?" Barbara asked, "Can't handle the truth?"

Jo rolled her eyes and tried to push me away from her, as Barbara continued to follow us, she continued to ask me questions.

"I asked you a question... are you mad that Abi has him now and you don't?"

As Barbara started to reprimand us, Abigail came by, she looked about as innocent as can be, but Jo and I knew the truth about her, knowing that it was not her persona. She came over to me and the first thing she asked me was to talk. I immediately turned away and ignored her.

"What is your problem?" Abigail asked

"I don't know maybe the fact that you're a homewrecker Abi. I never cared about the whole Richies thing, I never did, and you treat us like this." I claimed to her

"You're a little dramatic, don't you think? Oh right, you're just mad because Brian wasn't satisfied with you." She said to me, immediately I was thrown off guard. She also told me that I needed to satisfy his needs, and when is she going to realize that dating is not just about sex? Where does she come across when it comes to fooling around with other people's boyfriends, and she had one of her own, why doesn't she go sleep with him. Not my own. I have never been anything but nice to her, I never cared about who liked who, and the people on the other side of town.

"Stay a prude Evelyn, see if I care," Abigail said to me as she stormed off, she just could not handle the truth, the truth that she was in the wrong.

I heard the bell ring and I went over to my first class, and I didn't realize that he was in my class, as in Dean, the one that was cheated on by Abi. I felt bad for him I will admit it, but given his reputation with the girls, I am sure he had a one-night stand the night he found out. Jo was sitting next to me as Dean chose to sit behind me. Seconds passed and I heard my name being called I turn around and it was Dean, exactly who I thought it was.

"Don't even think about it." Jo pointed at him.

I didn't know what to say to him. His girlfriend cheated on him while he spent the summer in jail. What am I supposed to say about that? *How was jail? How did you find out about Abi? When did you guys break up?* I literally don't know how this works.

"Hey, Dean..." I said almost stuttering. I will admit it was nerve-racking talking to him, given how attractive and handsome he is.

"Look, can you meet me at the Rebel Pony tonight? At 7?" He asked me sternly.

Jo was surprised and I was shocked too. I could tell Jo was not liking the idea, or whatever he had in mind. I was confused. And All I wanted to know was why. Why did he want to see me?

"Look," Jo said, "I don't know what your deal is, but if you want to screw her or something you just gotta tell her."

"I actually just want to discuss business with her," he said with his cocky and arrogant smirk, "You know a game plan. To get back at Brian and Abi for what they did to us."

Oh? I didn't know what he had in mind but a part of me wanted to know what he was planning.

"Okay... count me in."

Jo gulped as she saw I agreed, she didn't know what was going on him my head. She thought something was wrong with me for agreeing to spend time with him. At The Rebel Pony, a bar that he lives in, teenagers in a bar is something that I always found dangerous and Jo didn't like the idea very much. She thought he wanted to get in my pants or something, and both of us could name five girls he slept with in the past months. But then I realized... He was in jail all summer. Jo knew I was a virgin and knew I wasn't going to put out for him. And she knew I wouldn't sleep with someone out of anger. It was all about the right timing for me, and after a breakup is never the right timing.

"And don't worry Jo..." Dean added, "I know what is going on in your head right now, and the answer is... Yes... she will still be a virgin after tonight... Unless..."

His cocky self wishes.

"You're disgusting," I said

Jo had a lot of dirt on Dean. He was arrested for the first time when he was twelve and had a criminal record as long as can be. He slept with almost every girl in town. Flirts with every girl that he lays eyes on. He definitely was a cocky eighteen-year-old. Of course, he could have any girl he wanted. He was handsome, charming, 6'2" with broad shoulders. With a bit of James Dean charm about him. One thing I asked myself.

Why was I doing this?

After class, Jo and I walked out of class and started to reprimand me for agreeing to be alone with Dean. Jo had senses on who he was... even Winnifred, who was walking past me with Julia and Jenny, was taking Jo's side.

"Talk some sense into your naive sister Winnie." Jo stated

"What is happening?" Winnifred asked.

"Evelyn has a Dean appointment," Jo said rolling her eyes.

"Jo is full of shit," I said, even though I knew she wasn't. I don't know if Dean was actually trying to pursue me or not, and I only was going to find out tonight when I am alone with him. Jo then started to mention the Rebel Pony and how I was going to hang out with him there. Julia knew he lived at that bar and Julia immediately jumped to Jo's side, while Winnifred and Jenny did not say a word.

"He can't be that bad," I said as I heard the bell ring and chose to walk away.

The night came around and I got myself ready to meet up with Dean. I put on my favorite pink floral dress, and my favorite headband to match. Why was I getting dolled up? For a boy. It was ridiculous of me to want to get dolled up for a boy. Especially if his name was Dean.

I went downstairs and I saw Trixie come into the house, rushing to get ready for her second shift. I needed to get away from her before she started asking me questions, but she caught me.

"You going out?" Trixie asked,

"Yeah. I'm just meeting with Jo."

I turned around as I heard Winnifred, Jenny, and Valerie all laughing. I turn around and all of them stop their laughter.

"Alright." Trixie replied, "Don't be home too late."

"Okay." I replied to her as I walk out of the house. I shut the door and turn around to see Winnifred and Valerie looking out the window I look at them both with annoyance and walk over.

I got to the Rebel Pony, the outside was a bit dark, with strobing lights and the Pony falling off slowly, I look through the window and I noticed that it was really crowded which freaked me out a bit. I knocked on the door and sighed... I didn't know why but I felt the butterflies all in my stomach. The breeze was letting my hair flow, it was getting cold.

The tall bartender, Mark opened the door for me, he had a beard and longish hair. A Black t-shirt and denim jeans and a denim jacket. He could tell I was too young to be in a bar, he looked at me and it looked like he knew. He knew I was there for Dean.

"Wait here." He said as he walked off. I looked through the window to see what happens at these things. There was a pool table, and another couple making out by the bar. I hear the door open and it is Mark.

"Come in." I followed Mark's orders and I went inside I sat down on the chair, and a man approached me. He had to be thirty years old, he wrapped his arm around me and I was uncomfortable with it clearly as he started to pursue me.

"Hey... she's with me." I heard a familiar voice say, I turned around and I recognized who it was. "Seriously. Back off." Dean was ready to fight him. The man was immediately afraid and ran off instantly. He took his hand out and I took it as he lead me into his room. I didn't think anything of it... was he going to... OH NO! As I got to his room with him. I was immediately stunned, dirty socks all over the place, it smelt like what a boy's room would probably smell like, odors and cologne.

"What's going on?" I asked, "What are you trying to pull?"

"Nothing... what are you thinking?"

I remained hesitant. I didn't want to say the wrong thing, I didn't want him to know that I think he is trying to seduce me. I didn't want to.

"Are you trying to seduce me?" I asked bluntly.

"You wish." He replied to me.

I didn't know what his plan was and I was slightly confused.

What goes on in this boy's brain?

"I had an idea." Dean stated, "We can pretend to have a relationship in front of Brian and Abi. You know a way of possibly getting back at them."

Hold it... Hold it now... Would they buy that? Would anyone believe that troublemaker Dean Richards is going out with me? I didn't understand. What did he think was going to happen with this "relationship". He was held back sophomore year of High School, Got arrested at twelve, and lost his virginity at fourteen. I on the other hand was a stranger to his world. I only would be out of the house for school, sometimes the drive-in, maybe a few rumbles, and possibly hanging out with my friends.

"Do you trust me?" He asked.

"Yeah," I said quietly, I was shivering.

"You seem a little reluctant."

"Sorry... I..."

"You listened to Jo didn't you?"

I nodded. Dean then looked at me and started to walk a little closer. He moved my arms away from my clutching stomach, I looked straight into his blue-green eyes as he looked into my blue ones. He had such nicer eyes than I thought he did... like wow... just gorgeous.

Evelyn. Snap out of it.

"You are in for a long ride darling..." Dean sighed, "Do you want me to take you home?"

I nodded. Dean is right. I am in for long ride.

CHAPTER SIX

Trixie

The first day of school was here, I woke up earlier than planned, due to having an earlier shift than usual. The girls were still upstairs, taking a really long time, which I definitely found frustrating. I was making breakfast for myself and the girls, and I made myself a cup of coffee as Evelyn came downstairs, she was earlier than she normally was, and immediately, she made herself coffee.

"Morning Ev." I said to her, she looked at me and smiled.

"Morning."

"How did you sleep?" I asked

"Better," she replied to me, I couldn't tell if she was still asleep or not since her voice sounded really raspy. Not her normal soft tone most of us were used to.

"You tired?"

She nodded and took a quick chug in her coffee. "I Got up earlier than normal," Evelyn said as she took another chug in her coffee. Evelyn never really made anything difficult for me, she knew how things were difficult and how things were never going to be easy again since we had so much that we had to deal with in the course of six months. She even tried to help as much as she could to make things easier for me.

Winnifred came downstairs about ten minutes after Evelyn did. She just sat down at the table, expecting me to cook for her like a princess. She had a book in her hand and started to read it, without even acknowledging us. Not me nor Evelyn. Winnie was a whole other story when it came to everything that we went through. But Winnie was a fourteen-year-old girl, of course, she was going to act like a teenager. Winnie especially was the one who made everything difficult for me, I don't think she tries to, she is having a hard time of course, and I am pretty sure she is still grieving. But everything about her just screamed angry teenager.... her mouth, the amount of time she wasted, I needed to be at work, and she just blatantly ignored that. Every single day.

"Winnie?" I said trying to acknowledge her as she was reading "Good morning?"

Not a word from Winnie.

"Winnifred..." Evelyn said trying to acknowledge her. Still nothing.

We heard the door open moments after only to see Valerie come barging in along with Paulette and Jo seconds after. Jo just started to eat as soon as she came in. Paulette raided the fridge with alcohol, I tried to protest them, but they were like family. I really couldn't say no to them.

Valerie just sat down next to Winnifred, putting her feet on the table like an animal.

"Val we aren't in a barn!" I said to her. Val just ignored me and chuckled. "Get your feet off the table. I'm serious."

Valerie looked at the sternness on my face and chuckled, she then took a second and put her feet off the table.

"Thank you." I kindly replied to her.

Jo was eating a corn muffin she found and Paulette got whiskey from the fridge.

"Can you guys raid someone else's fridge?" Winnifred said to both of them. As Paulette went in the fridge to get more Whiskey

"Most people need coffee in the morning, I need liquor," Paulette said. I took the second bottle out of her hand since I didn't want her to get into trouble. Or myself for giving underage kids alcohol. which could get me in trouble, and I could possibly lose custody of the girls.

"Come on, get to school," I said in a stern tone.

"Okay. Okay Mom.." Winnie said, "I mean Trixie."

Valerie chimed in before it got to the point where Winnifred and I were bickering, "What's the arguing about?" she asked,

"I just have to keep these two in line," I replied to the smart alec in Valerie.

Winnifred went with Valerie and left without a goodbye, and Evelyn left with Jo and Paulette, and I got a goodbye from Jo, Paulette and Evelyn. It was nice of them to acknowledge me, and all I have been doing for them to make sure they didn't get sent to a girl's home far away from this town.

I saw the envelopes of bills I needed to pay that were either overdue or due next week.

Goddamnit! Why is everything so stressful.

"Shit," I mumbled to myself. As I continued to look at the overdue bills, why was everything so difficult? It was more difficult than I thought. I went into raising these girls after my parents died, knowing the struggles, but it was better than sending them to a girl's home... right?

I heard the door knock minutes later. I look through the peephole to see Max Darling, Valerie's older brother, we met in high school and I was good friends with him, and his best friend Tom, who both clearly had a crush on me. He was in a similar situation as I was, raising his younger sibling, the difference was is that Valerie was closer to turning eighteen than Evelyn and Winnifred were so that just adds to the difficulties for me at least. But Max, he just had six more months. And Valerie swore to herself, that she was getting out of this place. So Max has told me, in regards to her.

"What brings you here Max?" I asked him, "Tired of Being a Protective big brother for a bit?"

"Just a smidge." He replied, "Valerie is still causing trouble,"

"How has she not been sent away?"

He shrugged his head and sat down to look at the bills that were still needing to be paid. He stopped looking at the bills and looked over to the newspaper.

"Mayor Albert Scott..." He said, "always in front of the newspaper... really making me mad everytime I look at that smug face."

"His son is no better..." I replied, "Like father like son."

Max chuckled and I chuckled as well. I explained to him what happened with him and Evelyn, and how he hurt her... hurt her... like really.... really hurt her. I've never seen someone so upset since our parents funeral...

"She should never trust anyone by the last name Scott!" Max claimed, "That just screams trouble and manipulation."

I chuckled again like I was in high school all over again... only this time I wasn't in high school... I was a twenty-one year old, who was having to raise a fourteen-year-old and a sixteen-year-old and I now knew what my parents felt like when I was that age. I knew this wasn't going to be easy. I knew that from the start. I was working at the hospital, so my two years at nursing school could come in handy...But why am I starting to realize that months going in that nothing was easy?

"How do you handle raising Val?" I asked him

"Val... is stubborn and never backs out from a fight, so it's hard... very hard I will admit that..." Max said, "But something about her is, she's a troublemaker, but she's not going out of her way to get arrested just to spite me, thank god because if she did that, she would be sent to a girl's home so fast... yes I did threaten her... once... or twice. But she still has a good heart and I know she wouldn't do anything to get me in trouble."

"Yeah I know Winnie and Evelyn wouldn't either, but Winnie is just so angry all the time and grieving... and Evelyn is always stuck in the middle of everything and I feel bad because I ask her how she's feeling and she never is honest with me." I replied to him, "They're both good kids... really good kids...."

"Well..." Max added on, "You are doing a good job."

"I'm trying." I smiled

I knew Max always had my back, especially since he and I had somewhat similar stories in regards to taking care of our siblings.... only Max has one alive parent, but their father is in jail...

"If you need help with anything," Max added on, "Give me a call... I'm a call away."

I nodded. As I put my jacket on to get ready for work. Max and I walked out of the door together and I hopped in my old car, and Max walked away... back to his house which was only a few blocks away. I started the car and waved to him as I saw him walking by. I knew he wouldn't leave my side.

CHAPTER SEVEN

Winnifred

Days have passed since the events of almost getting killed by the richies, I started to wonder what was going to happen when school started. Were the problems and struggles that we were going to deal with, and are dealing with ever going to go away. Nothing seemed like it was ever going to end. It wouldn't. It never would've.

Things were getting tougher, rougher, and harder on all of us.

I met up with Valerie the next morning and I started to walk with her to pick up Jenny. We walked to her door and we noticed all the lights were off, her parents were fighting, as usual. And I could not imagine what Jenny's whereabouts were. With what things were like with her at home, I just knew it couldn't be good. Jenny was going through hell, her parents were fighting because her father cheated on her mother. And Jenny. She caught him cheating. They still live together for financial reasons and they barely say anything, and sometimes when her father drunks too much, we could tell. So, he takes his anger out on her. And so does her mother. They both say that Jenny is putting a ruin to their marriage. It was her father's fault. Not Jenny's.

Jenny opened the door, and she had this giant bruise on the side of her face. Me and Valerie immediately knew that something wasn't right.

"Jen?" Valerie asked her, "What's this about? Where are your parents?"

"They just left for work."

"Damn it." Valerie muttered under her breath, "We will deal with this later. Let's go to school."

We both listened to Valerie and we followed her like a herd of sheep. She looked over at both of us, to make sure we were both okay. I was fine, It was Jenny, she was really worried about it, what Jenny's parents were putting her through. She hasn't said a word the entire way to school. She just nodded or shook her head and shrugged her shoulders whenever myself or Valerie had something to say. We both knew something was up. Things were not getting better at home and they were never going to get any better.

We got to school, and we saw Julia Rose, one of the Richies with her friends, I think their names were Cheryl who was the shorter one and Karen was the taller one. Julia seemed to like us since she did wave at me once she saw me. And of course, I waved back.

We walked past them and Julia approached me since we were in the same English class. Valerie and Julia hated each other, so Val rolled her eyes and Julia numerous times.

"Hey Winnie." Julia said to me as I walked over to her

"What's up?" I asked her

"Did you get the notes from last class?"

Valerie rolled her eyes as Julia asked me a question in regards of notes and schoolwork. Julia was one of the few richies I could actually tolerate, but Valerie, she didn't trust any of them.

"Don't let this richie pressure you into anything Winnie!" She shouted in front of Julia loud and clear.

"Just shut your trap." Julia stated in a very stern tone not caring what Valerie had to say, "I just need a few notes since I missed class... so get lost."

Valerie rolled her eyes. When it came to arguments, especially with the richies, Valerie always loved to have the last word. Even when she was in the wrong, which most of the time she was.

"Like I am so scared of this richie." Valerie snapped.

"You are such a bitch!"

Valerie heard the word 'bitch' and did not even look offended in the slightest, she knew she was cold hearted and didn't like to play the nice girl act, she just loved to open and up front with people and wanted people to know that she didn't like them.

"Wow..." Valerie said sarcasticly and not surprised, "Tell me something I don't know honey."

One thing that always admired me about Valerie is how she had no shame in who she was, I will admit I was afraid of her when I first met her, because of how cold and blunt she was, it made me wonder if she actually liked me at all. I look at Valerie stunned, I didn't want to tell her to 'cut it out' or 'leave her alone' because I knew she wouldn't try and stop being mean, especially if it was a richie.

"Look," Julia sighed, "I am actually asking for something in regards to an assignment, so can you do me a favor, be nice and let me talk to Winnie!"

Valerie made a few faces, we all knew she wasn't going to be nice, she hated being nice.

She just loved to continue to do what she did, and not cared.

"Well...." Valerie started to say, "I'm never nice." She walked off with a giant bird flip towards Julia.

"Sorry about her..." I said looking somewhat apologetic, but I wasn't surprised.

"Don't worry." Julia interrupted, "It's Valerie Darling what do you expect from her?"

I knew she wasn't wrong, and Valerie was someone that was not afraid to make a child cry. Or break into a bank, or terroize anyone, make a man cry, she just did what she did. And just continued to be herself. Which was something I knew I was worried about.

Then I look over to see Jo and Paulette walking with Evelyn. I had to know what was happening and why Jo and Paulette were putting crap on Evelyn.

"He's just using you Ev!" I heard Jo say to Evelyn,

Who is the 'he' in the situation? Was she thinking of getting back together with Brian? Because if she was, I would have to talk some sense into that girl.

"What is going on?" I asked Jo

"What is going on?" Jo repeated my question, "Evelyn went to hang out with Dean last night."

Paulette looked over and I could tell she was drunk... this early in the morning. But there was as definite that Paulette was following into everything that was going on.

"bad boy Dean wants Sweet Innocent Evelyn." Paulette said clearly intoxicated pointing at Evelyn.

Evelyn rolled her eyes, and I looked straight at her, Dean is worse than Brian. I mean Brian is a piece of shit, but Dean... was a whole criminal who was just released from jail.

"Evelyn, are you out of your mind?" I asked her.

"It's no big deal..."

Jo was stunned by her words, and I was equally as stunned. What the hell is going on in her mind? It is a huge deal. Dean is the type to sleep with a girl and then avoid her the next day. Dean is going to break Evelyn's heart. And she was incredibly naive and We all knew this about her.

CHAPTER EIGHT

Evelyn

Days have passed since we started the negotiation, I've been spending most of my time at The Rebel Pony, there were days when I pondered whether or not this was a good idea. If Dean was playing me, knowing his reputation. And knowing what kind of guy he was when it came to certain girls.

Was he playing me? Did he just want Abi back?

That was something I needed to figure out for myself.

I spent the past few days hanging out with Winnie and Jenny making sure they were alright as Trixie was at work. Just to give Trixie some help around the house. But I had a lot of other things on my mind, from Brian and Abigail getting together. To Dean's negotiation. It was all so much. I also had plans to hang out with Dean's friends, so that was something that was nerve-racking for me wondering how they were going to feel about me. I already sort of knew them from school. Stephanie was a little aggressive and was not afraid to speak her mind, while Jason was a little bit open-minded with a lack of knowledge and Derek was sweet, a nice guy, he had a massive crush on Valerie, and made it very obvious as well, so I wouldn't be surprised if there was a moment where he would talk about her. He tried to talk to her numerous times, but she just dismissed him, Every time.

"So, what are your plans, Evelyn?" Winnifred asked as I was no longer spacing out. I looked over to Winnifred and Jenny that were noticing that I was spacing.

"Hm?" I responded,

"I said what are your plans?" Winnie asked me again

"Oh..." I was hesitant for a second, wondering if whether or not I should tell Winnifred what I had in plan, "I... Am meeting up with Jo."

"Not Dean?" Winnifred asked in a smart, sarcastic tone. She definitely knew what really was in store for my weekend plans.

"No..." I stuttered, "Not Dean. Jo... and maybe Paulette."

Winnie started to look at me funny. And later looked at Jenny, who was starting to sense something. But I tried my hardest to deny what was really happening because I know Trixie would hate the idea of me being around a guy like Dean since Trixie always has had a hatred towards him. Maybe it's because Trixie dated guys like him when she was my age. She was always sneaking out to see certain guys, and she definitely rebelled against mom and dad. I remember all the times when she fought with mom and dad about who she was seeing. She had a Valerie phase at one point, which drove all of us insane, and maybe I guess she is worried that I will turn out that way. But I know who I am, and I know I won't ever change who I am. Especially for a guy.

"Well, Have fun, Evelyn," Winnie stated in a smart tone. "And be safe."

I rolled my eyes, I couldn't take any more irritation from my sister anymore. And her friends got involved. I'm relieved that Valerie wasn't there for all of this, because I know she would have a thing or two to say. Especially when it came to my love life.

"I will be fine girls," I responded to them.

I walked out and took off to the Rebel Pony. The Rebel was loud, with lights dimming like a regular bar would at that time. I walked in and Mark, the bartender noticed me, he was very confused on why a sixteen-year-old girl would be in a bar, but then realized I was probably there for Dean and pointed to the pool table, where he was with Derek, Jason, and Stephanie. Stephanie was almost like Valerie, but someone I was more afraid of, she was blunt, honest, and true to reality and wasn't afraid to say the truth, even if it hurt. Jason was like a golden retriever, he just was always happy and Derek was one of the most down-to-earth guys I know. He was really sweet, kind, and genuine plus seemed like he actually cared about his friends, hoping they wouldn't get into any trouble. The first one to notice me was Stephanie, I could tell she wasn't too happy about seeing me because she rolled her eyes at me the second I walked in. I never thought she liked me, and that particular moment made it all obvious.

Stephanie tapped on Dean's shoulder, pointing at me, Dean looked over and waved at me. He seemed like he was happy with my presence. But Steph, not so much. Jason and Derek looked over and it seemed like they were almost surprised at my attendance. I walked over and greeted them.

"Hey..." I said in a quiet tone.

Stephanie looked over at me and started to examine me almost, to see if maybe I was safe. Or maybe Dean's type.

"Want a smoke?" Stephanie asked me.

I shook my head.

"No, I'm okay." I replied

"She's not that type of girl Steph," Dean stated.

"Should've known," Steph said and went back to the pool table. Jason smirked and Derek whacked him for staring. Derek reminded him that it was rude to stare. Dean walked over to me and started to make me feel welcome.

"Can I get you anything?" Dean asked

"I think I'll sit for a bit," I replied. Dean sat down next to me.

"You playing?" Derek asked Dean. Dean shook his head, he seemed like he actually cared about my safety and my whereabouts. Did he? Or was he playing me?

"She's too much of a good girl." I overheard Stephanie saying to Jason. Jason seemed like he wasn't paying too much attention he just cared about beating Derek in the game of pool. I couldn't tell if Steph was intimidated by me, or if she just didn't like that I was around. She was always to be considered the type to keep her emotions in, something that I always noticed about her.

"Don't worry about her." Dean said to me slyly, "She's a jealous bitch sometimes!" He said louder. Stephanie looked at him and gave him the bird. I laughed only because it was similar to Winnie and Trixie's relationship. Fighting like typical siblings do, It was always funny.

"Do you think you'll be okay with her?" Dean asked me, as I nodded, "Okay she's a bit to handle. But we love her anyway, every night after school we usually hang out here. Just after homework." I nodded at this, this was going to take a lot to get used to. And on top of that, I had family that I needed to hide all this from because if Trixie found out I was seeing Dean, she would be against it whether it was Real or Fake.

"I usually need to be out of here by 10:00 on weekdays and 11 on weekends," I told Dean.

"Don't worry. I will make sure you do." Dean replied in a sly tone. It seemed like Dean loved to tease me, maybe it was because I didn't fit in with the rest of his friends or maybe because I was seen as "too innocent" for the rest of his friends. Maybe Winnie and Jo are right, I am a little too naive sometimes.

"What's the matter Ev?" Dean asked,

"Nothing." I said.

"Nothing?" He asked, "Are you sure?"

I nodded.

Dean pulls me upstairs to his room.

"Where are we going?" I asked and he silenced me to shut up.

He brings me into his room and shuts the door.

"What are we...." I said as he started to interrupt me, I was gonna ask him if he was planning on doing something with me, but he wouldn't let me finish.

"No. No. No. We are not going to. I am an excellent liar, we can pull it off." Dean stated, "Look kid, I wouldn't do anything to you without your permission, I may be a jackass but not Brian's level."

"Okay..." I said silently. All of a sudden Dean starts to move a little closer to me.

"We just need practice," Dean stated.

"Practice for what?" I asked,

"You know....school.... so people believe we actually did this shit."

I wasn't believing any of this. Dean Richards. Was so close to me that I could not imagine it. His dark eyes and the thought of him close to me, like I couldn't imagine. He was handsome. I will agree with that, any idiot could see that about Dean. He was tall, dark, and handsome, and anything a girl could want, but he was also bad news. I knew I couldn't give into that as I pushed him away.

"I should probably go." I said to him as I grabbed my sweater and ran off. If I fell for him, that would lead to trouble.

CHAPTER NINE

Trixie

Max tried his best to make sure Trixie was hanging in there, and she could've used as much help as possible. After all, Trixie kind of needed it, she had bills that needed to be paid, while working two jobs, one by volunteering at the hospital and just recently started working at a diner to get a little bit of extra cash. Max cleaned the table as Trixie got ready for work.

"Go. I'll take of it." Max claimed.

"Are you sure?" Trixie asked, he just nodded and signaled her to go to work.

Trixie did exactly that, She walked right over to work. She mouthed the words "Thank you" to Max and left, she was grateful for

Max, grateful he would help her, mainly because he was in somewhat of a similar situation that she was in, having to raise their teenage siblings, only Max still had a living parent who was MIA, but actually just in jail for some sort of armed robbery, but that was all she knew about what happened since Max didn't really want to talk about it.

Trixie got to the hospital and knew that she was running late, but luckily she made it just in time. She was lucky. Lucky That her boss hadn't found her running late. Because that would have been the third time in that week. Her friend Patsy who had just graduated from nursing school helped her blow her cover, and make sure that she wasn't caught by her boss, who took work at the hospital seriously. Patsy was always loyal, she was optimistic and true, even in the worst times, while Trixie was a little more pessimistic, which is one of the reasons why they started to click so well. And the reason why they became such good friends.

"Rough night?" Patsy asked

"Yeah. Girls are teenagers, one is fourteen and the other is sixteen so of course, they're going to be causing a little bit of trouble, but still, they're good kids at the end of the that just had a rough time lately coping with the death of our parents."

"Fair, Which one do you have the most trouble with?"

Trixie knew she was having problems with Winnifred, she was just always talking back and having a little bit of anger towards her. While Evelyn, tried her best to stay calm as possible but how long was she going to keep it up until she cracked?

"Winnie probably. She's angry." Trixie said, "Evelyn's fine I just feel like she's sort of caught in the middle of everything, she's sweet and I just feel like we constantly take advantage of that, that's why I think I worry about her all the time."

Patsy could empathize with Trixie and with everything that she is going through, she had to grow up fast and had to drop out of school to look after her sisters, it is better than being sent away to girls home, it was better than them being sent away and never seeing her sisters again, it was hard, it was hard to stay out of trouble and not get involved in fights with the richies, with the rivalry with the Richies getting even more intense, and Patsy knew that everything was getting harder and harder by the minute, especially with this being the time where the girls would act up around this age. Trixie had a hard time and Patsy and Max were the only ones that could understand that. They could understand what she was going through and admire her courage and bravery during her tough times and Trixie was stronger than she thought. Patsy and Max knew that. They knew that Trixie could do anything.

CHAPTER TEN

Winnifred

I needed to clear her head that night. It was a Friday night so I wanted everything to be a mind-clearer, not thinking about fighting it out with the Richies, and the family issues that I was trying to move past. I needed to get her friends away from all of it. And what better way to do it, than by going to the drive-in. There was some old western movie playing and I had a good feeling that Jenny and Valerie would have fun. Valerie could definitely sneak them in without having to pay, she was always good with that.

I knocked on Jenny's door first, since Jenny lived closer to her house, I figured it would be the easiest. I knocked on the door and Jenny opened the door quietly and snuck out.

"Hey."

"Hi."

"You ready? Do you want to go grab Val?" I asked her.

Jenny nodded.

"Alright, to Val's house."

Jenny and I walked over to Valerie's house and we spent some time talking before we got there. We went from one topic to another, we just didn't want to talk about out family drama, and the battles with the Richies for once in our lives, as we got to Valerie's door, I knocked on it, while Jenny was behind me. Max opened the door

"May I help you two?"

"Hi. Is Val around?" I asked Max, Max always thought we were intimidated by him, but we never were. Valerie ran immediately as soon as she heard her name come out of my mouth, it was almost like she was ready to leave.

"We're going to the drive-in," Jenny said.

"Great. I could catch a movie." Valerie replied.

Max looked at Valerie and started to give her a big brother look.

"Val. 11:30 curfew. Because If anything happens to you... you know what can happen." Max stated in his protective big brother voice.

"What do I do when something happens to you?" Valerie asked him trying to fight back since she was not afraid to fight back or get the last word, especially if it was her own brother.

"You see," Max started to reply "I don't let anything happen to me."

Valerie knew that wasn't true, she knew that things have happened to him in the past, but she wouldn't let him get the last word, and Valerie, she loved to get the last word in, especially when it came to arguments with her brother. So she let a certain word slip her mouth.

"Bullshit!"

"Alright wiseass," Max demanded, "11"

"I was joking." She said jokingly and somewhat sarcastic, she really didn't care because she knew he was joking about the curfew, Max didn't care too much about a curfew, he just cared that his little sister was safe, and he didn't want her to end up like her father.

"But seriously, 11:30 is curfew." Max said, "Try to be there."

"I know." She said flipping him off and she walked off me Jenny and I.

"Thank you Max." I said to him walking off.

As we got to the Drive-In Valerie got us under the gate so we didn't have to pay. It worked, it worked every time, because, Valerie hated paying and she hated people and hated talking to people, she hated a lot of stuff, especially the Richies. Jenny and I went to go sit down as Valerie went to get us popcorn and probably slash Derek's tires like she usually did. In order to get him to stop flirting with her, hoping he would've gotten the hint years ago. So while we waited for Valerie, We spent time waiting in silence for her until we saw some people we didn't want to see.

"Oh...Shit." I said as I saw Brian Scott, with his minions, Abigail Jackson, Sandra White, Karen Thompson, Barbara Keller, and of course, Julia Rose. Julia was one of the few Richies I liked, so she wasn't one I was too worried about in regards to causing problems because she hated this rivalry almost as much as I did. So if anything were to happen she could try and stop it. Valerie came back with popcorn with us and as soon as she saw the Richies, she was not pleased. So she sat next to Julia to really bug them.

"Val.." Jenny said, hoping it would stop her from doing anything that she'll regret. But she immediately turned over to Brian.

"You got some nerve asshole," Valerie said to Brian. Those were the kind of words that Jenny and I were afraid of. But it's Valerie, of course, she is going to curse people off if she doesn't like someone, "I'm friends with Evelyn man. And her sister... And you treat her the way you did."

Brian was stunned, he started to act as if nothing happened, and everyone was starting to notice it, including me and Julia. Jenny, Julia, and I all tried to tell her to 'cut it out' or 'leave it alone' but she always would refuse to listen. Valerie just did what she wanted without any shame of the consequences, sometimes her behavior would get her in trouble, but she took it with a grain of salt and moved on with her life. Which was something about her that scared me a little bit. Sandra added on the fact that she was looking for a fight, and Valerie knew that, she loved to fight, which was something the whole town noticed about her.

"Look if you were a guy I would knock your teeth out," Brian called out.

Valerie chuckled, she wasn't scared of him, she has beat him up several times before so she wasn't scared of him at all.

"I could slap you," Abigail added on, which added fuel to the fire. Because many Richies could scare Valerie, and she still wouldn't be scared. Especially the Richies. As Abigail got up from her chair, Valerie continued to sit down pretending to be scared to death.

"You rotten little..." Abigail said to her as Valerie got up.

"Whatever you say, homewrecker. After what you did. when my friends are hurt I'm gonna defend them. It's not like you'll do anything."

Abigail was surprised by her words, Abigail was also acting like she didn't ruin a two-year relationship. "You have no right to call me a homewrecker, all because Brian cheated on Evelyn. You better leave us alone..." I was surprised to see Abi deny everything, who was the other woman in the situation, Abigail was.

"Or what Abi, did you cheat on him yet? Because I can name everything wrong with all of you. You all won't fight, because you're scared to wrinkle your fancy dresses." Valerie said chuckling because she knew she could beat all of them up in a matter of seconds, one wrong move, and their dresses would be wrinkled. And probably all of them would end up coming home with a black eye.

"Brian, get out, you're making me nauseous looking at your ugly face!" Valerie shouted at him, "You too Abi Get out of here!"

Paulette came in to sit next to me and Jenny, asking what was going on after Brian and Abigail left and we explained how Valerie is picking fights with the richies. Brian and Abigail had a terrified look as they were almost running away from us.

"You just love to pick fights don't you?" Julia asked her,

"Now you're just noticing. How bout this Julia. I think you're annoying..."

Julia was never afraid to fight back in a battle with Valerie, because she had a mouth, she may be sweet but she was someone you didn't want to cross.

"Go to hell Val!" Julia shouted.

"Oh...Honey, I already have a free ride." Valerie said in a confident tone.

"Guess what, you should stop because I am this close to calling the cops." Sandra said trying to chime in and hoping that Valerie would be scared.

"Oh my. My goodness. Do you really think that scares me?" Valerie said in a sarcastic tone, they really thought they would be able to scare Val with the 'I'll call the cops' threat, Val has been in Juvie several times, the other delinquents and officers knew her by her name "Winnie you got the keys to the cuffs with you right. What? Have you guys seen my record?" Karen tried to give her the bird, and Valerie responded with two.

Valerie then got up and said she was going to get more drinks. She pulled a flask out of her denim jacket and walked off. Paulette, Jenny, and I all looked at each other. Julia, Karen, and Barbara looked at me while Sandra gave us a look too.

"You know," Jenny said, "Val's not so bad once you get to know her."

"I'm sorry," Barbara responded, "The last thing I would want to do is get to know Valerie Darling. She is an accident waiting to happen."

I couldn't believe those words. She wasn't a bad person, and nobody could really see that. Valerie had a good heart, she had just been hurt too many times.

Minutes passed and Valerie returned handing over drinks to me, Paulette and Jenny. Later giving the richies drinks. She licked one of them and gave one to Karen, spit in two of them and gave them to Barbara and Sandra. Until she spilled Julia's all over her.

"You damn Idealistic," Julia shouted standing up, she was not afraid to fight back and was ready.

"What?" Valerie stated, "You need to cool off anyway."

They started bickering for a few seconds, until the Drive-In manager came in to ask what the issue was. Valerie immediately sat down, hoping Julia would get in trouble.

"Julia Rose just started fighting me." Valerie said in her lying voice, until Julia mentioned how she got the stain on her dress "As for the dress, that was an accident. Daddy can buy you a new one." Valerie added on.

"Come on Val." Jenny said, Valerie was refusing to say a word. Until Jenny stood up.

"Excuse me." Jenny was about to speak until Valerie tried to protest, "Valerie started the fight."

"Seriously?"

"Alright." The Manager stated. "Julia, Valerie, you're both out."

"Are you kidding?" Valerie said angrily, Valerie hated when things didn't go her way, "Way to go..."

The Manager escorted her out, and later Julia. Valerie was definitely annoyed that she didn't win a battle. But I always know that she wins the wars. Because she can fight, especially in rumbles. But Valerie was not afraid to get back at them, especially in school on Monday.

CHAPTER ELEVEN

Evelyn

I got to the Rebel Pony, and it was like a party like it always was. It was crowded, I sat alone by the bar and Mark seemed to be a little bit annoyed by me. As I sat down for at least two minutes, Dean, Stephanie, Derek, and Jason were all at the pool table. I tried not to make eye contact with them, hoping Dean would notice me first. But it was taking him a while to notice me, too long. Longer than I hoped. I was really hoping Dean would see me, and greet me, but he was too busy with those friends of his.

"Here for Dean?" Mark asked, "You usually aren't his type. No offense."

"Yeah, I am," I replied to him.

"His type is usually more...sluttier," Mark said, "You know what I mean."

I nodded, I understood exactly what he meant, he knew Abigail and how she hurt him and was more of the slut type. Abigail was a perfect example of his usual type.

I felt something tap on my shoulder, as I turn around I see Dean over to me, I sat in silence and he seemed somewhat confused, about why I wasn't moving or talking. I didn't want him to know what Mark said, but Mark is right, I am not usually the type of girl that he brings home to the bar. I was completely different, his friends didn't like me too much, which scared me a little bit, wondering if they were gonna crack me. If they were going to do things that I was not too familiar with, such as smoking and drinking. But I know that nobody would force me to do anything that I wasn't too comfortable with, especially Dean.

Dean walked with me to the pool table, the first thing I noticed was Stephanie smoking, the smoke was in my face and she continued to make sure more smoke got into my face, which was an immediate sign that she didn't like me too much. While Jason and Derek were trying too hard to beat each other with pool, not even paying attention to the fact that I was there with Dean.

"Want one?" Stephanie asked offering me a cigarette,

"Oh, I'm alright thank you," I responded when she knew I didn't smoke.

"Should've known." Stephanie responded in a snarky tone, "Whatever. I doubt you could handle a drink either,"

Immediately Dean rolled his eyes at Stephanie, and Stephanie looked over at him and was starting to get annoyed by him. She didn't like me, and I knew that it was clear from the beginning that she didn't like me, I could understand why too. I wasn't the type that she usually hung around. I guess she considered me someone that she would never trust, but that's okay because not everyone is going to like me in this world.

"It's one cigarette." Jason added, "And a drink."

"Jason. She said no." Dean added, "You should respect that without being a little shit."

"Really? Evelyn I'm sorry that you can't handle anything..." Stephanie added on

"Shut up Steph!" Dean added

"God I hate her." Stephanie mumbled

"Tough!" Dean yelled

Dean was defending me, I didn't understand why, I was just an ordinary girl joining in with the fake relationship thing, and I was hanging out with him and his friends, Dean barely noticed me in the past. He walked over to Stephanie because he was almost fed up with Stephanie's constant remarks.

"Hey. Give her a break. What the hell has she ever done to you?" Dean asked, "She's a really sweet girl, you would know that if you gave her a chance."

Stephanie rolled her eyes and was just stunned by how much he was defending me, I was watching it all occur as the boys were arguing over who was winning the game of pool. I spent time watching Dean argue with Stephanie. About me. What was so special about me? I was just like every other person... from the south side of town. I was just trying to belong, find my place in the world like everyone else on the south side, trying not to be overlooked by the richies. Stephanie knew who she was and she never really seemed to care what anyone else said, and she was always blunt and made it known if she disliked someone, without caring if that person disliked her.

"Look at her! She's this little virgin Mary who thinks she can just come in here and do whatever she wants..." Stephanie said almost throwing a hissy fit and jumping out of frustration. Stephanie walked over to the pool table with the boys.

"I'm sorry about her," Dean said

"Don't worry," I said, and I started to look over my shoulder, to later notice something I wasn't expecting. Trixie with Tom. And Max.

"Oh my gosh," I mumbled

Dean was confused as to why I was so nervous until he looked over and saw Trixie. I was surprised to see her, and so was Dean. Of course, Trixie had a life, but I never would expect to see her over at the Rebel Pony. I tried my best to distract myself by playing pool until I heard her call my name.

"Hi Trixie," I said in a scared nervous tone. Trixie walked over.

"What the hell are you doing here?" She asked angrily and Tom walked over with her. I pointed over to Dean and Trixie was not amused to see that Dean was there with me.

"Why is she with you?" Trixie asked him annoyed

"Because I said so," Dean replied,

Trixie tried her best to not get violent with Dean, because she knew if she could, she could beat him up in a heartbeat.

"Ev, say goodbye to Dean." Trixie said before she did anything that she would probably regret. "I know all about Dean Richards. let's go. Why the hell didn't you tell me you were seeing him?"

"Because..." I said, "Because I...."

As Trixie dragged me away from the Rebel Pony, Tom and Max went with us outside to the car, I was mortified and shaken with embarrassment. I wanted to stay and I just didn't want to be treated like a kid all the time. I couldn't take it anymore. Trixie is even more controlling than she was when Mom and Dad died, and I was over it. Beyond over it.

"Look, Dean and I are just friends. I really wish you can just give him a chance even if we weren't together!" I said in a frustrating tone.

"He's bad news Evelyn, If you weren't so stupid you would know that he is not a good person." Trixie said, not realizing what came out of her mouth, "Evelyn I didn't mean..."

I just sat quietly, things were just frustrating. Since mom and dad died I wasn't getting as much freedom as I wanted. But what did I expect? Trixie was too controlling and having her belittle me too. It was too much.

"Forget it." I said, "I just want to go home."

CHAPTER TWELVE

Trixie

I spent so much time working, working more than I would usually in the span of a week. So this weekend I got fewer hours than I normally would. Which was convenient for me, so I would have time to rest. Or do whatever. I sat down on the couch and turned on the TV, there was nothing good playing. So I got up and made myself some food and went to sit by the TV again hoping something would be on. But still nothing, so I ended up with a Tweetie Bird cartoon, I always liked those as a kid. Watching it reminded me of childhood, reminded me of the fact that I am not a child anymore. Which was sad. But I had to grow up fast, I didn't get to complete college like I hope I would have, and I now am working on raising teenagers, it was hard because they were moody teenagers and they were hard to deal with, but then again that was like, life was filled with obstacles that I needed to face. Hours passed and the door knocked, I wasn't expecting anybody to come by, so I had a slight confusion as to why anyone was coming by. I open the door to see Patsy, looking almost like Valerie.

"What's going on?" I asked her.

"You and Me are going to the Rebel Pony tonight," Patsy said, happy and bubbly. Thinking I was in the mood to go to a bar. Especially on my day off, "Your day off you should be having fun."

I rolled my eyes, knowing that Patsy was not going to stop until I agreed, but she was right, I needed to let loose. But part of me would have rather wanted to stay in, and catch up on sleep but another part of me wanted to let loose and be a normal twenty-one-year-old girl.

"Alright," I sighed, "I guess it would not hurt." Patsy smiled as she heard those words, I barely remember the last time I went out with my friends all together. I'm pretty sure the last time I did it was a little before my parents died, I was still in school, so I actually had a life. Patsy went inside as she waited for me, Paulette came in. It was a little random for her to be dropping in, then again Paulette practically lived her sometimes.

"Hi Patsy." Paulette said coming in invading the fridge, "Trix? Do you got any twinkies?"

"Yes, bottom drawer," I replied, as I went upstairs to get changed.

Minutes later, I come downstairs to see Paulette with a beer in her hands and twinkies.

"Jesus Paulette, are you trying to get me into trouble?" I asked her,

"No..." Paulette said with a twinkie shoved into her mouth, Paulette never had a problem with making a mess in the household. It was one of her specialties.

"Paulette, I'm heading out. I'll catch you later and don't drink anymore."

Paulette nodded and Patsy and I left the house.

We got to the Rebel Pony, and saw Max by himself, we sat next to him and we were pleased to see him. And Max was pleased to see us as well. I took my first drink in six months and it felt great being able to have time to spend with my friends and have time for myself. But a part of me was also nervous about what was going to happen while I was not at home. I didn't think they would cause trouble, but it was probably me overthinking.

"So, you like being a mother?" Patsy asked,

"I don't know how my mother did it." I said, "It's exhausting. "You know, Winnifred, she's taking all these advanced classes, how does her brain not explode. Evelyn, is still trying to keep everything together, for me and Winnie. You know, sometimes when I see Evelyn, I think of Mom."

I didn't actually realize how exhausting this whole process was going to be for me. My parents didn't even warn me about it, but again they died pretty suddenly and I had to be a parent overnight. But they are great overall, Winnifred was always a little bit of a smartass and Evelyn is a bit quiet, it was always like she wanted to say something but she didn't want to. She was always like mom, she was kind and gentle and was always nervous to say the wrong thing. My mom was always attracted to the wrong kinds of people until my mother met my father, they were actually happy again, they both went through rough patches. But they helped each other through it and ran away together.

"It's so crazy how different all of you are. Evelyn's sweet and you're this annoying little..." Max started to say until I whacked him in the head. Patsy laughed, she thought it was so funny how we bickered.

"You two fight like you're a married couple." Patsy chuckled, "Do you want to go play pool or something?"

Max and I both nodded, and Patsy got up and tripped immediately because she was tipsy and leaned on Max. I laughed watching, I thought it was always funny how easily drunk Patsy got. It wasn't good, but I found it entertaining from the stories Max told me.

But as I got to the pool table, I noticed something that really caught my eye, and it really surprised me.

"Evelyn!" I shouted, as she turned around in fear and Dean turned around with her.

"Hi Trixie," she said in a scared nervous tone.

"What the hell are you doing here?" I asked angrily and Max walked over with her. I pointed over to Dean and Trixie was not amused to see that Dean was there with me.

"Why is she with you?" I asked him annoyed

"Because I said so," Dean replied, Dean's wise-ass sarcastic tone was really making me angry.

I tried her best to not get violent with Dean because I knew if she could, she could beat him up in a heartbeat. And of course if we fought, I would win. So before anything happened, I dragged her away from the Rebel Pony and Patsy followed us back.

We got outside and I let Evelyn into the car, and she was not happy. She went on this whole rant on how none of it was a big deal and how I should not get upset over her hanging out with Dean. She kept saying that he was a good person and he just was misunderstood, all that bullshit, I heard it all before. Evelyn was naive. But scarily naive.

"He's bad news Evelyn, If you weren't so stupid you would know that he is not a good person." I yelled at her, but moments passed and I was not realizing what came out of my mouth, "Evelyn I didn't mean..."

"Forget it," She said, "I wanna go home."

CHAPTER THIRTEEN

Winnifred

After the drive-in, Jenny and I walked home with the Richies, it was actually fun getting a chance to spend time with them and forget about the feud for once. Julia was so nice, and so were the other girls. Paulette joined us also to make sure we got home safe, and if they were going to pull any stunts. It was actually fun getting a chance to get to know them, they all seem different without Brian and Abigail around. Julia seemed like she actually cared about me and my family, she cared about what I had to say.

"How are your other sisters Winnie?" Julia asked

"They're good, Evelyn is sneaking around with Dean," I told her. Julia seemed surprised, she could not imagine Evelyn going to see Dean, but a part of her was also not surprised at the same time.

"How did they end up together?" Julia asked,

"She won't tell me," I added, I never actually knew how they met and how they ended up together, but life was filled with unexpected things to occur. Especially with romance and who we fall in love with.

Julia saw her stop and saw that there was a car, the richies all went into Barbara's car, and all of them waved to the girls, myself, Paulette and Jenny all walked back to Jenny's, and the first thing we heard was her parents fighting again, Paulette immediately took Jenny under her wing and told me that she was gonna let Jenny stay at her place for the night. I lived close to Jenny so I walked back and they went to Paulette's. As I got to my house, nobody was home. I went upstairs to bed. I got into my pajamas and crawled into bed and started to read Catcher in the Rye. Minutes passed and I hear the door open, I must have assumed it was Trixie coming home, or Evelyn, and all of the sudden I hear arguing. I recognized those voices immediately. I saw Evelyn come into our room and she slammed the door, I have never seen her annoyed or upset like this at all.

"What's going on?"

"Ask Trixie!" Evelyn shouted and ran to the bathroom, "How humiliating!" I heard her mutter to herself.

Trixie came in and mouthed "Dean" and I was confused, did she see them together or something.

"I caught them at the Rebel Pony," Trixie said as Evelyn came out of the bathroom. I looked over and started laughing. For once it wasn't me getting into trouble or getting yelled at by Trixie. I thought it was entertaining for me. To see Evelyn finally do something rebellious. I never thought I would leave to see the day.

"Wow. Evelyn Martin Rebelling." I teased, Trixie looked at me and pointed at me not to make it more of a big deal than it already was.

"We'll talk about this in the morning," Trixie said to Evelyn in a stern tone, as she left, I couldn't help but let my laughter out of my system. Evelyn looked at me and told me not to laugh. She didn't like how I and Trixie made this a big deal, because to her, it wasn't. It really wasn't. But to Trixie, it was a big deal, only because she didn't want us to get into any trouble. Especially if it was trouble that Dean Richards would get her into. I told Evelyn I was going downstairs because I needed a glass of water, I did exactly that, I walked downstairs into the kitchen and got the glass of water I needed. I chugged the water since I was dying of thirst, thinking about everything that had been occurring in the course of the past few hours. From Valerie getting into the fight with the Richies and later hanging out with them to Evelyn going to the Rebel Pony, all of it was just an eventful experience to witness.

Minutes passed and the door knocked. I was confused, mainly because I didn't know who would come to our door at this hour. Maybe it was the police or a social worker. But it was two in the morning, a social worker wouldn't come then. I opened the door and saw something I didn't want to ever witness. Jenny, she was bruised and black-eyed and had a scar on her arm, my heart almost shattered seeing her.

"Jenny...Oh my god." I said in a hurt tone, "Where's Paulette? What happened?"

"My parents happened, I got yelled at for staying out too late, they ordered Paulette to leave and my dad hit me a few times, I couldn't fight back Winnie. Why couldn't I fight back?" Jenny cried, "My dad is an angry drunk and my mom just watches it all happen."

Trixie came downstairs, asking me who was at the door, and the moment she saw Jenny, she ran down the stairs, ordered Jenny into the house by pulling her in, and shut the door. Trixie examined her face, to see what was happening to her, Jenny explained everything to Trixie, the way she explained it to me. Trixie couldn't believe any of it, she wanted to report her parents, but then Jenny would be sent away, or have nowhere to go. But Jenny's safety was the first priority, for all of us.

"Jenny..." Trixie stuttered, "I am probably going to report your dad."

"Please. No. Don't." Jenny sobbed, "Trixie Please. You can't."

"Jen, he's abusing you. What else am I supposed to do?" Trixie asked

"Trixie," I added, "She doesn't have anyone."

"And Besides, I have two more years left." Jenny said, "One in a half almost. Let's just leave and when I turn eighteen I can get justice."

"Are you sure?" Trixie asked. Jenny nodded. Trixie cared about Jenny just as much as Valerie and I did, and she hated seeing Jenny hurt, that is what hurt her the most, knowing that she couldn't help out Jenny.

"What are we going to do?" I asked Trixie,

"I don't know, But Jenny is staying with us for a bit," Trixie said

"I would hate to intrude," Jenny replied,

"Jen, you're like my sister. Of course, we are going to look after you." I said, "But we are going to deal with this."

"Just don't let Val know about this." Jenny cried knowing that Valerie would get arrested for beating up her father for beating up Jenny.

"We won't. I promise." Trixie said

CHAPTER FOURTEEN

Evelyn

Thinking about Jenny getting beat up by her parents threw me really off guard, I never knew how bad her home life was, and how badly her parents were treating her, I could not imagine everything that she was going through, because I knew there was an issue with Jenny's parents before ours died, because mom and dad always told us if they could, they would adopt Jenny. And everything that happened tonight, was the wake-up call, that things were getting really bad, quickly.

I didn't realize it at first, but it wasn't just with the Richies, but it was everything around us. Our families were getting ripped apart, and anger was getting taken out on us. That's what it must have been, with Trixie, Jenny's parents. God only knows if Max was doing the same thing, but Valerie always fought back, especially with her brother.

I saw how hurt Jenny was and I wanted to keep my distance, I tried to help but I was getting more upset seeing Jenny broken the way she was. And it pained me too, just anyone in pain hurt me. I felt horrible, everything we went through felt like nothing compared to Jenny.

I went upstairs to think, think about how bad things were going to get eventually. But I just had to clear my head. As I laid down on my bed, I heard the knock on my window. I look over to see Dean himself. What was he doing here?

"Dean? What are you doing here?" I asked him opening the window

"Hey. So after you left, I did something incredibly stupid," dean started, "so after you left, I fought Brian and challenged him to a rumble!"

"Dean.. You did WHAT?" I was shocked but also not at the same time, of course Dean and Brian's rivalry was getting more intense. But I never thought would ever get this far.

"I couldn't help myself... I sort of was feeling angry." Dean stated, "Because of obvious reasons."

I couldn't get mad at him, he was Dean, after all, there was never a time where he wasn't mean or being a hothead or starting a fight, that was something I admired about him. He was very cute though... *Oh my god... Evelyn NO!*

"So when's the rumble?" I asked him

"Tomorrow night." Dean said, "Tomorrow night in the alley where we always have our rumbles. We're going to need the best fighters we can get."

"Can I fight?" I asked

"Ev, it's too dangerous." Dean said, "I just don't want you getting hurt."

"Do you think I'm that weak?"

"No, I just..." Dean started to stutter, I've never seen him like this, he crawled into my room from the window, "I just can't watch you get hurt because you're too fragile, have you fought in these before?"

I shook my head, I always wanted to fight in rumbles but Trixie never let me or Winnie. He was right though, I let my guard down easily, rumbles are usually for girls like

Valerie, Valerie could beat anyone up, she intimidates not only the girls but the guys.

"I think maybe this can be my chance to prove myself." I said,

"I don't know if that's a good idea!" Dean in a louder tone, "I can't have you hurt okay, this was me, all me..."

"I think it would make sense if your problems are my problems,"

"Why?"

"You and I are...well fake of course..."

"You're right, why do you even care?"

"It's my job to care."

I didn't think I was going to start to care, but I did. Dean and I had something going on, fake or not fake, I still cared about Dean, even if he didn't care about me. Because I was seeing him every day, and what we had was something.

"Look, Ev, You're different from Val, Steph, or even Jo." Dean said, "And honestly I kind of like that about you."

"Okay..." I said silently, "I won't... I promise."

"Thank you!" Dean drawled.

I had to keep my promise, to Dean. Because Dean wanted me safe, and I don't think he would be happy if I fought in the rumble, as much as I wanted to he was right, I wasn't ready yet. Not in my wildest fantasies, I was too physically and emotionally vulnerable, he knew that and I knew that.

"Dean..." I stuttered, "Why do you care?"

"I have to care, as you said."

"Evelyn." I heard Trixie say walking in my room and opening the door, seeing Dean, her face turned ghost white, I had a feeling her reaction to seeing him again would be angry after seeing him with me at the rebel pony, so I wasn't surprised by her immediate reaction, "What are you doing here Richards?"

"I just came to bring Ev her sweater," Dean lied,

"Yeah, I'm sure," Trixie said, "Get out now Richards, Jenny is hurt and we don't need anyone else getting hurt."

"Jenny's hurt?" Dean asked sincerely and almost worried, "Why didn't you say so? Is she alright?"

"It was a fight with her parents." Trixie said, "Not like you give a shit."

"Is Jenny alright Trixie?"

"Yeah, Winnie and I have been looking out for her for the past hour," Trixie said, "Seems like you've been keeping Evelyn busy?"

"Dean only just got here, he came here by surprise," I said trying to defend Dean,

"I was just telling her about the rumble tomorrow Trix," Dean said and then realized what else he said, "Also, the sweater."

"Rumble?" Trixie asked, "Another?"

Dean and I nodded at the same time, we knew that this rumble was going to be bad. I wanted to fight so badly, and I know Winnie wanted to as well, but I had to look after Winnie, even though I knew Trixie was going to fight as well.

"Count me in." Trixie said, "I want to fight."

I was surprised but also not at all, Trixie loved fighting in the rumbles because it was everything in her youth and everything she did in high school and everything she had before she became a mother overnight. One of the reasons I admired Trixie, she had mother instincts and was not afraid to fight someone if they crossed her.

"You sure Trixie?" I asked

"Yup." Trixie said, "Now Dean If you want to help with Jenny, that would be great."

"Yeah, no problem," Dean said, I was pleased that he was willing to take care of Jenny, it shows how much he actually cared, deep down I knew he cared about all of the Idealistics, especially the more fragile and vulnerable ones. Like me or Jenny.

CHAPTER FIFTEEN

Trixie

Jenny wasn't getting any better, her home life wasn't getting any better either. Along with that, we had a rumble to prepare for, I couldn't believe that Dean did that, got us in the middle of his rivalry with Dean, and I cannot believe we are involved now, but it isn't really anyone's fault, Why do I keep blaming Dean for all this? Because it was also Evelyn's ex-boyfriend as well. But I couldn't blame her for all this either. Because I shouldn't blame her either. It is not her fault either, she couldn't have done anything to cause it all. Dean challenged them to the rumble, not Evelyn.

Things were getting bad, and getting worse by the second. I didn't think much of any of it, but my sisters were involved and they were friends with girls that picked fights and hated the ones that picked the fights with them. But I didn't want to let my sisters get into any trouble, because if they got into any trouble I knew that a Social Worker would take them away. And I sure as hell did not want that to happen. I don't know what the future was going to be in store for everyone, but I didn't want the girls to get involved in the rumble because that was the last thing they needed. I didn't know what I was going to do, there was enough shit we had to deal with. But the main focus was making sure that Jenny was alright.

"Alright, I am going to go take care of Jen now." I said, "We will talk later."

I went downstairs to check on a shaken Jenny as Winnifred stayed with her making sure she was calmed down. And As I was taking care of her, I noticed Dean coming downstairs leaving, and Evelyn brought him downstairs to the door to let him leave. I looked at both of them and gave Dean a dirty look and as Dean left, Evelyn came by to help take care of Jenny. And so did Winnifred, I brought over things that would help her keep her comfortable, like a pillow, blanket, and a warm towel for her head. We let Jenny rest and lay down on the couch, and she gently took a few deep breaths with Winnifred almost was on the verge of tears, she hated seeing what her best friend had to go through and knowing it was getting worse for her by the second, and I hated watching my sister upset, especially when one of her friends was going through hell, especially when one of those friends was like a younger sister to me.

I looked over at Evelyn who was looking over at me, I didn't know what was going on in her head, but this Dean Phase of hers needed to stop because it was going to end badly, and I knew that if something bad were to happen because of Dean, I would be the one that would have to take care of her, and I had enough on my plate.

"Alright, we have to discuss the rumble." I said, "Because it is sitting in my constantly, I'll fight in the rumble,"

"Are you sure Trix?" Winnie asked me

"Yeah, I know Dean and Valerie are definitely going to fight."

"Do you want me and Evelyn to fight?"

"No. Over my dead body." I claimed, "Neither one of you are fighting, if you guys argue with me there will be consequences."

"Why not?" Evelyn huffed

"Because I am not interested in social services sending you to a girl's home."

Evelyn agreed and so did Winnie, Jenny also didn't want to fight either. And she made that clear, and Paulette and Jo would not let her either to begin with because they knew how fragile Jenny was.

"what's going to happen now?" Winnie asked

"I have no idea." I responded

CHAPTER SIXTEEN

Winnifred

The next morning, I woke up extra early to make sure Jenny was safe. I looked down and that was the most peaceful I saw Jenny sleep on the sofa, I stayed sitting down on the chair next to the sofa, and I smiled, Trixie came downstairs calling for me and I signaled for her to be quiet.

"Is she still asleep?" Trixie asked,

"Yeah." I responded, "No way I want her fighting in the rumble."

"Good, because she's not." Trixie said, "And neither are you."

"Why not?" I asked standing up

"Because it's dangerous I am not interested in seeing you get hurt, end of discussion."

"So that's it?"

'Yes, that is it."

I wanted to argue with her as much as I could, but there was no point. Trixie put on her jacket and left for work, and I rolled my eyes at her. And saw Evelyn come downstairs.

"Did you hear about the rumble?" I asked her

"Yeah I did." Evelyn answered, "Dean challenged them to one."

"Of course he did. You and this infatuation with Dean are really getting old."

Evelyn rolled her eyes and went upstairs. I couldn't help but laugh as she went upstairs, and Jenny slowly started to wake up, I turn around and heard her call my name. I immediately rushed to her aid.

"Are you alright Jenny?"

"Yes, I'm alright." Jenny sighed, "I'm a little tired."

"I know you are honey."

I hated seeing Jenny upset, she had so much that she was going through and so much that she had to deal with. With her parents, and a bunch more, Jenny did have the biggest heart of anyone I know, and it pained me to see her in pain. I didn't realize how bad her parents were making her feel. And it started when her dad cheated on her mom at the Rebel Pony when Jenny was going to visit Dean and Dean caught him cheating on her mom, and he has been taking it out on her ever since because she immediately told her mom, that they stayed together for financial reasons and they are always fighting. Most of the time when her parents were fighting, Jenny would stay at our house, most of the time she would have days where she would lay under the covers all day and not go home, her father started drinking even more and that only resulted in more anger from her father, she fought in a few rumbles and could really fight, which surprised most of us, especially Valerie. Who was always doing anything to protect Jenny, and so was I. And we never stopped caring and we will take care of her until the day we die.

"Did you hear about the rumble?" I asked

"Another rumble?" She asked silently, "We already had three in the span of a month!"

"I know, you and Evelyn aren't fighting, Trixie won't let us, but I'm fighting anyway."

"Are you sure that's a good idea?" Jenny asked, "You can get Trix in loads of trouble."

"Yes, I'm sure," I responded. I then stood up and went outside for a little bit and let Jenny know that I was getting a little bit of fresh air, then I saw a face, a face that surprised me a bit, It was Julia Rose. I would have never believed anyone if they told me she was outside our house, but she was. While Julia got there, Paulette came running into the house, which wasn't unusual for Paulette.

"Winnie?" Julia asked, "Do you have a moment?"

I nodded, I would not have minded talking to Julia, she was one of the few richies I actually liked talking to. So, she definitely was going to help us maybe, I just thought it was odd that she wanted to talk to me the day of the rumble.

"I heard about Jenny, is she alright?" Julia asked

"Yeah, she's staying with us for the night."

"That's good." Julia responded, "Are you going to be at the rumble?"

"Hopefully, if Trixie gets the stick out of her ass."

Julia chuckled, but she looked down a little bit, maybe because she felt bad, felt bad that so much was happening to us, The Idealistics in particular. Valerie, Jenny, Me, Trixie, and Evelyn while Paulette and Jo had to take care of us.

"Try to be careful, if you go in the rumble, okay?"

I nodded and agreed, Julia did care about my safety a lot, which is one of the reasons I admired Julia so much. She was always really sweet, and she wasn't like the rest of the Richies. Which was great.

Paulette came back outside and went down the steps of the house.

"Is everything alright?" Paulette asked with a twinkie shoved in her mouth.

"Yes, everything alright, she's just warning me about the rumble tonight," I responded. "No weapons tonight, so nobody can get killed. Thank god, and Brian and Dean are going to go head to head."

"Oh, interesting. Brian and Dean are going to finally fight. I am so ready."

"I'll see you guys tonight," Julia chuckled and walked off, as she left, Valerie walked by and Julia rolled her eyes at Valerie.

"Take a picture honey, it'll last longer," Valerie said,

"Go to hell," Julia said walking off.

Valerie walked over to me and Paulette and sat down on the stoops and started laughing. Paulette and I looked over at each other and then looked over to Val, who was staring at us, she looked a little different too.

"What's up with you?" Paulette asked,

"Oh I got into a fight with Stephanie no big deal." Val responded, "Anyway, want to get Dairy Queen?"

"Why?" I asked,

"Because she was bad talking Evelyn last night at the Rebel Pony, so do you guys want Dairy Queen?"

Jenny walked outside and Valerie smiled and walked to her.

"Jenny, how are you?"

"Better. I heard Dairy Queen." Jenny responded.

"There it is..." Valerie chanted and clapping her hands, "Winnie, you coming?"

"I guess I don't have a choice,"

"Paulette?"

"No thanks." Paulette responded,

"Okay?" Valerie said, "Missing out."

Valerie then hopped in her car, even though it wasn't actually her car. It was Max's.

"Is that Max's car?"

"Yes, not stealing I'm borrowing."

Jenny hopped in the car and I went in the back while Jenny took shotgun. Valerie started the car and started speeding the car pretty fast, at one point she was running into mailboxes, which really got all of us intimidated, and then she started to take her hands of the wheel, as we were close to Dairy Queen, she started speeding faster and complaints were being said and cars were honking.

"Are you trying to kill us?" I shouted.

Then we finally reached the drive-through and Valerie ordered for all of us. Milkshakes, chocolate, in particular, fries, and coke. Really weird combination but people would assume Val is a healthy eater, but she really isn't. As we got our food, she parked the car, in the parking lot, and Valerie just laughed, she turned around and saw two guys and winked at them.

"Alright? Everyone happy?" Val asked, "Got away from the folks for the day, we got a nice rumble that we are going to win."

"I'm thinking about fighting in it." I claimed, "I'm going to fight in the rumble actually."

Valerie turned around and was almost stunned. Jenny looked at me in a "you said something dumb" look, I couldn't help but chuckle. The only word that came out of Valerie's mouth was "NO" she wasn't going to let me fight, I knew that because she spent her life protecting me and Jenny, but I wasn't a kid anymore, and Valerie needed to understand that I didn't need her protection anymore.

"Winnie, Trixie going to kill you," Jenny said

"Yeah, is your stupid ass trying to get sent to a girl's home?"

"No."

"Then don't fight in the goddamn rumble."

"I don't think you get it..." I said

"I certainly do." Valerie interrupted, "Everything that Trixie does is to keep you safe and you are going to run around and do your own thing? NO! Not gonna happen, okay?"

Jenny and I just remained silent, Valerie has gotten mad before but not like this, I didn't actually realize how the Richies were causing a lot of trouble for us, but I didn't understand why I still couldn't fight, nobody was using weapons and I wasn't going to get stabbed or shot, and if I stayed by Dean or Valerie I wouldn't have an issue.

I am not a kid anymore, and she just didn't get that.

No one did.

CHAPTER SEVENTEEN

Evelyn

I spent most of the day alone, trying to figure out what was next. Obviously, there was the rumble, but I was trying to figure out what was going to happen after the rumble. To start off, there was definitely going to be something happening, whether it was to me or Winnie, but if anything happened to us, we knew Valerie would hurt them viciously.

I always had a somewhat fear of the rumbles, because the rumbles were always deadly, and sometimes people would get hurt permanently. I know some people years ago weren't able to walk again after getting brutally hurt at some rumbles.

I spent some time over at the Rebel Pony, hoping to get some rest and get my mind off the rumble, I didn't want any alcohol or anything I just needed a place to sit down and relax other than my own home. I spent time sitting down and I noticed that Stephanie was sitting down next to me, that was a very interesting site for me to see, especially when I thought Stephanie hated me.

"Hey." I heard come out of her mouth, I turned around and said "Hey." Back and I smiled at her.

"You fighting in the rumble?" She asked me,

"No...are you?"

"Yeah," Stephanie responded, "So are you here to see Dean?"

I shook my head, and I mentioned to her how I came here on my own. I started to look around and see if he was at the bar and I didn't know it. I looked at the bruise on

Stephanie's eye, and it looked like she got punched in the face.

"What happened to you?"

"Valerie Darling beat me in a fight is what happened."

"Oh," I said, it was a bit silent in our conversation for a couple of seconds.

"You're not drinking?" She asked

I shook my head and mentioned that I didn't really drink that much. But then Stephanie smirked, and I didn't know why and asked her what it was about.

"I see...you don't do much of anything" Stephanie sighed, "...I don't know how Dean's into you..."

I was somewhat confused about what Stephanie had claimed, there was no way Dean was into me, especially since Dean and I made an agreement that we weren't going to fall for each other no matter what the circumstances were.

"Oh, you didn't know, Dean has a little thing for you. He's actually made it quite obvious." Steph added to her claim,

"How do you know?"

"You really wanna know?" She asked.

I nodded, I needed to know for sure if what Stephanie was saying was true.

"I probably shouldn't be saying this but...as his best friend, I know more than you would even think. Sometimes even more than what Jason would know, because if Jason knew he would probably forget to keep his mouth shut. And well...me, I know it all. But with you around it seems like you're fucking clueless." Stephanie claimed, and then looked up and down at me, and then paused and started staring at me.

"I'm not that clueless." I added, "I just sometimes don't realize things,"

"That's the literal definition of clueless hun," She said,

"Is there anything you want to add, about Dean?"

"But it's Dean. He's had several hookups, and he has some trusting issues because well...Abi was his first real girlfriend. He was never disloyal to her and he got backstabbed. Sometimes he has a hard time admitting and expressing himself easily, since he feels like anyone he's ever loved turns on him." Stephanie said, "He has a secret soft side, that he never really wants to admit, and honestly...He talks about you...a lot...too much to me. It makes me sick, how much he talks about you."

I couldn't believe the words that were coming out of Stephanie's mouth, it couldn't possibly be true, I didn't think this would ever happen to me, especially with the way my trust issues were, especially when I was with Brian, they got bad. But I didn't realize how bad they were.

"What does he say?" I asked trying to figure out the truth.

"Well he starts off, with whenever I insult your virgin ass, he'll defend you instantly. Saying "Steph Stop. She's not that bad!" or something like "Steph, she's not that innocent" or "she's a sweet girl." Makes me sick...but anyhoo, he also tells me that you're different...from other girls." She added, but I didn't understand, how could I possibly be different from any girls. I mean I wasn't different from any girl he has ever hooked up with, and they were pretty much all the same, and every girl he hooked up with, he has deflowered them, maybe that was what he wanted with me, just to deflower me. I don't know. Maybe I was thinking too much.

"I mean...you don't drink, don't smoke, you're loyal to those you care about, and to the ones who don't give a shit about you. Dean sees that. I think he's just scared. I don't think it's of you, however, just scared to screw up what he has and wants with you."

"And what could he want with me?" I asked her,

"Personally I think he wants to trust you, like I said before is a rough obstacle. He's always had a hard time trusting people. And I think deep down he does trust you but like you said...it's just a way to get back at Brian and Abi."

"Yeah, I know... But I am starting to develop something," I told Stephanie instantly regretting what I was saying. I don't know why I said it to Stephanie, of all people, the girl that is close friends with Dean, she was definitely going to tell him.

"Then say something," Stephanie said to me

"I don't know."

"What's holding you back?"

"A lot of things, myself, my family, what if I get sent to a girl's home?" I started to think about all the possibilities of what could happen in the course of the next few months.

"Try not to think about that," Stephanie said, "This is about you, not your family, not Brian and Abi, only you. And you can't really control who you fall for, and you can't really control how people feel about you. So I would say tell him how you feel before it's too late because if it's too late, you're going to wonder a load of what-ifs."

I started to sigh, and started to think, Stephanie was right, I did want to live my life with no regrets and I cannot control who I fall for. And I knew that Dean couldn't really control it either. I really needed to think, about me. And what was going to happen, I didn't know if I waited until before or after the rumble.

"Tell dean I'll see him after the rumble." I said standing up and running off. I immediately saw dean and I was about to head out of the door, which only encouraged me to run quickly.

I walked out of the Bar and turned around and looked over to see dean chatting with Stephanie. I didn't know what the conversation was about and I sort of wanted to know as well, but it wouldn't be polite to ask because it wasn't my place. I just walked back home.

As I got back home, I opened the door to see Trixie, Jo and Paulette get ready for the rumble I saw Winnifred and Jenny sitting down on the couch and Trixie ordered me to do the same. I sat down quietly and asked what this was about.

"We gotta a rumble tonight." Jo stated,

"And we're fighting in it, and Vals gonna meet us in the alley."

I turned around and saw Winnifred roll her eyes. And Paulette noticed it too and laughed.

"Alright. We're heading to the rumble now," Trixie said, "Please do not leave this house, Ev, you're in charge."

I nodded. As Jo, Paulette and Trixie walked out, I looked out the window and saw them all walk to the alley where we had our rumble. And I needed to know what was happening, but I didn't want to fight in the rumble.

"Ev?" Jenny asked "do you think everyone is going to be okay?"

"I think so, we got excellent fighters." I said , " and besides we got Dean and Valerie I think we will be just fine."

" I wanna fight now." Winnie claimed

" I know you do but Trixie said we can't and I am not interested and going to a girl's home."

" but I fought in the rumbled before," Winnie claimed, " and I've kept so many of these girls asses and I can do it again,"

" I know but things are getting bad around here and I really don't wanna lose you guys especially you"

Winnie cross her arms and rolled her eyes and started At Jenny, then gave me a dirty look. She wasn't getting off Scott free.

" I gotta use the bathroom is that okay," Jenny asked I nodded Jenny up went upstairs and Winnie followed her

"can you tell me why you're going upstairs?" I asked

"Just going to my room like a prisoner." Winnie claimed.

" OK but stay with Jenny please." I added. Winnifred follow Jenny upstairs I didn't think too much of it. Until I heard a sound of a window being shut 10 minutes later. I called for Jenny after she went to the bathroom Jenny came downstairs and I asked her what that sound was she didn't know. Jenny ran upstairs and I followed her I looked in our room and I looked in Winnie's bed to see if she was under the covers and all I saw were bunch of pillows and then I saw the window open and then I knew.

" Winnifred Grace Martin you are so dead." I claimed.

CHAPTER EIGHTEEN

Trixie

We started to walk over to the alley and I looked over at everyone that was there, and to me, it seemed like we had an amazing group that was going to help us win the rumble. I haven't fought in a rumble since Mom and Dad died and I was finally going to do what I

doing. I missed being a teenager, and I missed having a little bit of fun, and I forgot about the thought of me being robbed of my youth and my early twenties. I remember when I fought in Rumbles back in High School, And I was a Richie for a little while until I changed my mind and chose to hang around the Idealistics only because I found them a lot more amusing and the girls that were Richies just kept bullying them and kept bullying me and ruining my self-esteem. And also a part of it was because of my sisters, thinking if my sisters wanted to see me as one of the snobby Richies. Seeing me behave in a rude manner to girls that don't really deserve it. But not one part of me regrets my descison I enjoyed hanging out with them, and I felt like I could protect them in a way.

As we got to the Alley, I looked over and saw that Dean and Valerie finally got there also I saw Stephanie which really got me excited because I knew we were going to have a good chance at winning this. I told myself to try and be civil with Dean because everyone knew that I really disliked Dean. Dean smirked at me when he saw me but I couldn't help but roll my eyes, I didn't understand why he had to be in the picture, maybe it was because Evelyn was in love with him and she didn't want to admit it. I saw it, Winnie saw it and Dean probably saw it too.

Valerie looked more pumped than ever she had her favorite leather jacket on and she had her favorite boots on she was excited and she was ready to rumble. Valerie was sprinting to the alley, ready to beat someone up, but when was she not excited about beating someone up. Also joining us at the Rumble was Jo, Paulette, myself, Max, Stephanie, Dean, and Jason, who have a great track record of helping us with winning the rumbles. Valerie and Dean were cheering with excitement for the rumble, ready for the Richies to finally pay for the damage that was done. The damage towards my sisters, and their friends.

Meanwhile, I was still a little anxious and still a little nervous about the way the rumble was gonna turn out, and I was still looking around thinking about my sisters wondering where they were and if they were going to be

OK even though they weren't exactly fighting. Maybe I was just getting too paranoid. We waited for a couple of minutes for the Richies to finally get to alley and they finally got to the alley after waiting too long. Valerie and Dean looked at each other and the both of them crossed their arms and Abigail and Brian got in front of their faces, Valerie just looked over at Dean and smirked. And Dean was surprised that all of them even showed up. Especially Brian, who was secretly intimidated by Dean, almost like all of the guys his age did. So he wasn't too worried, he wasn't too worried about how this rumble was going to play out, because one wrong stare could make Dean run. But I still hated Dean, because he's just too snarky and cocky, and he is so obsessed with my kid sister, and I don't like it. At all. It makes me sick.

Once Brian and Abigail continued to stare at Dean and Valerie, it was silent for at least thirty seconds, and they both felt like someone had to say something. So Valerie was the one who was going to make the first comment.

"Took you long enough," Valerie smirked, "You guys scared to lose."

"Please Valerie." Abigail smirked, "You think I'm afraid of you, you guessed wrong."

Valerie chuckled, she knew that Abigail was afraid of her.

"I'm not scared to lose, and I'm certainly not scared of you." Abigail added

"Or were you too scared to get your dresses dirty?" Valerie said talking dirty and trying to get them angry, which was something she always did, especially before a rumble, "Oops. My bad. Oh, wait. You forgot about the fact that I don't actually care. Because, you all look too pretty for a rumble... with the pretty jewelry, fancy dresses and your hair in pretty little curls. Why didn't you dress more appropriately?"

"Val, cut it out." I said hoping she would stop, "You're gonna instigate things and it's all going to get worse."

"It's already bad enough." Val added, "Abigail, how many men have you slept with this week? 10? 20? 40?"

"Oh Valerie Darling, you are just plain rotten." One of the other Richies said I'm pretty sure her name was Karen or something, "You are a rotten little bitch,"

"I know," Valerie chuckled, "I mean, it is a rumble after all, in about a few short seconds you're pretty dresses will be all muddy and you'll be crying to mommy and daddy. Isn't that right Julia... oh wait, she's not here..."

Abigail was ready to attack Valerie until Brian shoved her away to make sure she didn't do anything stupid before the rumble.

"I really wish I could kill you," Valerie said as I tried my best to hint to her to cut it out, but she refused to listen, her brother Max, also tried to get her to cut it out,

But Valerie just smirked and made a few more snarky comments. Jo pushed Valerie away to make sure she didn't do anything. But Valerie always loved a good warm-up before a rumble. She was willing to fight all day long if she could.

"So, are we gonna start this rumble or what? Because I am not interested in just sitting around here all night long, I came here to fight and that's exactly what I am gonna do." Valerie said,

"Do rules apply tonight or..." Another Richie asked a short little blonde girl whose name I couldn't remember. One of the girls even claimed that she had a curfew.

"Hey. You don't need a curfew on rumble nights," Jo claimed, "Curfew is when we are done, end of the story."

Valerie and Dean nodded agreeing, that there was no such thing as curfews for them, especially on the nights of Rumbles. It was almost like the two of them were the same exact person.

"Can we get started already?" I asked, "I got two younger sisters that are waiting for me."

"Yeah, let's just wait for Valerie to finally decide to shut her mouth." Another richie claimed, "She just keeps running her goddamn mouth."

Valerie looked at me and she just started laughing, She was ready to get this rumble started. But then all of the sudden, I heard a voice, a really familiar voice that shouted "Hold on, I'm here, I'm sorry for the delay." I turned around and looked, I couldn't believe who it was. It was Winnifred. I couldn't believe my eyes. And as I got distracted by Winnie showing up, I felt a fist coming to my jaw, and I fell to the ground. I looked up and saw one of the richies standing up and laughing at me.

"Hey, what the hell?" I shouted, "I am an adult,"

"Then why are you here old lady?" She asked, "Besides, were all a bunch of teenagers."

I looked over and saw Winnie and Valerie teaming up against Abigail, I wanted to chime in and get Winnie out of the way and back home, but I had two other Richies standing near me and ganging up on me. I could definitely take them, especially since both of them were way shorter than me.

"Told you I'm strong! I'm stronger than all your lazy ass boyfriends!" I heard Valerie shout lifting Abigail and throwing her down on the ground and punching her, "Oh no! Now your dress is all muddy. What are you gonna do now? Go cry about it."

I ran over to punch Valerie when she was about to Punch another Richie but instead, she ended up punching me.

"Valerie!" I shouted, "I'm on your side, remember that?"

"Sorry Man." She rolled her eyes at me, I looked over at Winnie who was with Valerie, "You go home! Now!"

"No way!" Winnifred ran off and saw Brian, I watched her get onto Brian's back and watched as Valerie started beating him up. I looked over and watched everything get out of hand, and that only made me think less about the fight and more about my baby sister's safety. I looked over and noticed Jo and Paulette teaming up to attack a few Richies and Dean helping Valerie with beating up Brian, and then Stephanie and Jason going against two other Richies. And one of the Richies complained about their dress being muddy, and it got Jo and Paulette excited.

I turned around and I heard Dean, beating up Brian even more brutally than before.

"That's for hooking up with Abi" I heard come out of Dean's mouth and punch him again.

"That's for hurting Evelyn." He shouted and punched Brian again and then tackled him and threw him over his shoulder and then I heard something else come out of Dean's mouth.

"And that... is for threatening to hurt her. " He couldn't. He couldn't possibly care about her.

"She's not good enough for you, Dean." I heard Brian shout back and that got Dean even angrier, "What, are you mad that I was being honest? She's more into guys like me. Not low lives like you."

"You broke her! I hope you're aware!" Dean yelled at Brian, and that was something I was for once in my life agreeing with Dean about, "And i'm sure she spent every chance she got being enough but she wasn't."

"I regret wasting those years on her," Brian claimed, and boy that not only made Dean mad, but it also made me angry as well, I walked over and just gave Brian a giant punch in the face resulting in him falling to the ground.

"I knew you'd warm up to me one day." Dean smirked at me, I rolled my eyes and pointed at him,

"You hurt her and I'll kill you, But I still don't like you." I added,

I ran over to check on Winnie lying on the floor and I pulled her up.

"You okay?" I asked her then snapping out of it so I could scold her, "What is wrong with you? You shouldn't be here!"

"Good to see you Trixie." Winnie said laughing.

"It's not funny."

"Do not lecture me right now! I need to finish what I started." Winnie shouted running away to fight more Richies.

"Do not walk away while I'm talking to you!"

I turned around, and I heard sirens in the distance. It couldn't be. The sirens were getting even louder and louder.

NO. It couldn't be.

"Shit." I heard Valerie shout, "It's the cops. Run!"

Valerie, Jo, Stephanie, and Paulette ran as fast as they could followed by the Richies and then Dean, Jason, and Stephanie.

"Winnie run." I shouted for Winnie hoping she would run. But then the cops got there and it was too late, Winnie was the one in handcuffs.

"Alright, let's go kid." The cop said taking her into the police car, as she got thrown into the police car, I knew I was in a lot of trouble with Social Services.

This was going to be really bad.

CHAPTER NINETEEN

Winnifred

I didn't think the cops would catch me.

This is bad.

This is really bad.

Trixie is definitely going to be mad at me, that's for sure.

We could now get sent to a girl's home, and it is all my fault.

Maybe Evelyn and Trixie were right.

Going to the rumble was a bad idea.

Now I am in jail

And It could affect my permanent record.

Affect my future.

I'm fourteen.

I can't have my life ruined already.

These were all the thoughts I had as I was sitting in my jail cell, a bunch of other girls was all hanging around and playing card games, along with that heard two girls arguing at the cells across from me. I was laughing at their arguing when I really shouldn't have been laughing or that was going to definitely cause a bit of attention with them onto me, and I don't like causing problems and I definitely don't like my attention either, especially in dangerous situations like this.

"What are you in for kid?" The girl in the cell across from me asked

"I got myself involved in a rumble." I answered

"Oh, so you're one of the Idealistics, I've heard a whole lot about you guys, you guys have gotten arrested for a lot of things, do you know Valerie Darling?"

"Yes, she's one of my best friends."

"Should've known, she's gotten arrested a lot, I don't know how she didn't get sent to a girl's home yet."

I chuckled because she was sort of right, I don't know how she didn't get sent away either and say that Max was a bad guardian or something.

"What's your name?" She asked me

"Winnifred Martin." I responded, "But you can call me Winnie if you want."

"Hi Winnie," She said, "My Name's Scarlett."

I waved at her, she sort of almost reminded me of Valerie in a way, her mannerisms, her attitude, I could tell this was not her first time in jail.

"What are you in for?" I asked Scarlett.

"Armed robbery and arson," Scarlett answered, "I was here for a long time, that's all I am gonna say to you."

I laughed, and I wasn't intimidated by her like I thought I would be, probably because I was surrounded by Valerie for so long. But Scarlett has done way worse than Valerie, and the way she acts, seeing her fight with people in her cells, sometimes she made Valerie look like Evelyn. I sat down and looked around, wondering how long I was going to be in here, and thinking about how Evelyn, Trixie, and the other girls were going to react. One thing I knew was that they were not going to be happy with me at all. I looked at the gross toilet and I started to feel nauseous.

"Are the toilets always like this?" I asked Scarlett. She nodded. I then felt myself starting to feel sick and puked right in the gross-looking toilet.

"Are you okay Winnie?" Scarlett asked

"Not really," I responded and she noticed how pale I was, "That's disgusting."

Minutes passed and a police officer came by to my cell and unlocked it.

"What's going on?" I asked,

"Someone is here for your bail."

"Who?"

"Come with me please."

I followed the Police officer and he followed me to the station and I saw Julia.

What was she doing here?

"Heard you needed a bail." Julia said,

"How'd you know?"

"Word goes around easily," Julia said, "And I figured I might as well be a friend and not a foe."

"Thank you." I said, "I'm just nervous about how Trixie is going to react when she sees me,"

"Well..." Julia sighed, that sigh was different from other sighs, and I knew what it meant, "Trixie is outside,"

Julia walked outside and I followed her outside, I got down to the steps with Julia and Trixie was standing in front of her car. I knew this was going to be bad the moment Julia left, as Julia started to walk home she wished me good luck. Trixie asked her if she needed a ride and she said it was okay, and Trixie thanked her for bailing me out. I just hopped in the car before Trixie did. She looked around and then got into the car and just looked at me.

"Well, I'm glad we won the rumble right." I said, by looking at Trixie's face, I knew she wasn't happy.

"Just wait until we get home Winnifred," She said, "We will talk then, okay?"

I sighed and was getting nervous, I was sick of her constantly treating me and Evelyn like children, it was going to be the same lecture we always get, how everything was about her and she has nothing and we were going to be sent to a girl's home if we didn't shape up. I wasn't going to let them send me to a girls home.

As we stopped the car, I noticed that we were finally home. I looked at her and noticed that she didn't say a word to me, which got me a little bit nervous, thinking about how she was going to react. I opened the car door and then got out of the car and slammed the car door hard and ran into the house. I got inside and saw that Evelyn was sitting down.

"Hey Ev," I said, "Where's Jenny?"

"She went home."

"You sent her home Evelyn...after what happened are you stupid?!" I yelled at her

"It was her call," Evelyn responded, Trixie, came inside and slammed the front door. And I just looked at Trixie not saying a word. I also tried to not laugh either, otherwise, it was going to add fuel to the fire.

"Say something." I said, "Anything."

Trixie chuckled and rolled her eyes. She definitely had a thing or two to say and I just wanted the words to come out of her mouth.

"Are you kidding me right now? Seriously?" Trixie asked angrily, "You could've gotten yourself killed!"

I knew I wouldn't get myself killed, I knew Trixie got mad but not like this, this was different than any of our fights. I still didn't understand the big deal, we fought in loads of rumbles before, all three of the Martin girls, and this time we can't, was it because of Brian, was it because he was causing problems for us.

"I'm a big girl now, Trix." I said, "I don't understand the big deal."

Trixie clenched her fists together trying her best to control her temper, maybe I shouldn't have said that but it had to be said.

"You're 14! You're my kid sister! You're my responsibility now, what don't you understand?" Trixie yelled, I felt like I had to fight back.

"What I don't understand, is what YOU don't understand is the fact that you're not my mom! She's dead, Trixie, so stop trying to be her!"

Shit, maybe that wasn't the right thing to say. But it had to be said. Evelyn was getting a little distressed and I could tell by the look on her face. She wanted to calm us all down, but no one was getting calm.

"This is absolutely unnecessary right now," Evelyn said, "Are you kidding me?"

"I am sick and tired of you throwing mom and dad in my face! Who do you think you are! I didn't ask to be a parent!" Trixie said victimizing herself, like she usually does, "Damm it Winnie! Who's registered as your guardian? Me. Who pays for this house? Me. Who fixes the problems you get yourself into! It's me! All of it! Me!"

I was so sick of Trixie making every one of our arguments about her, and about how mom and dad were dead and she didn't sign up to be a parent. I was not going to let her win that easily.

"You know what, if I'm such a problem to you, maybe I don't wanna live in *your* house any longer!" I claimed, but she knew I didn't actually mean that, I just wanted to get a reaction from her.

"Right there just shows how immature you are. Yeah run away from your problems Winnie instead of working on them!" Trixie said then looking at Evelyn, "Help me out here, Ev. Tell her how ridiculous she's being!"

Evelyn looked at me and Trixie and she didn't say a word. She definitely didn't want to get involved. "Can you two leave me outta this?" Evelyn asked, and Trixie continued to argue with me,

"Winnie. I am trying so hard just to keep everyone in line, keep everyone safe. Even some of your goddamn friends, who come in barging in all the time." Trixie scoffed, I scoffed back at her, she was yelling at me too much. For what? Standing up for myself, taking a stand on what I believe in. It was too ridiculous. SHE WAS BEING RIDICULOUS.

"I can't believe you're yelling at me." I scoffed at her stomping my foot.

"Really, because you disobeyed my rules after I said not to go to the rumble... Winnie, you need to grow the fuck up... do you wanna get yourself killed?" Trixie asked, "God... why are you this ignorant?"

"Talk some sense into her Evelyn..." I said looking at her, "Come on, back me up."

"Goddamnit You guys, you know I hate it when you are arguing," Evelyn said, "Seriously, let's just not do this right now!"

"Do you wanna end up like Mom and Dad?" Trixie asked me, "Because you will if you keep acting this way... you will, and I am not taking care of it."

Okay, that was too far.

"Why would you say that?" I asked running up to my room. I looked over and noticed Evelyn was upset too. Things were getting worse.

CHAPTER TWENTY

Evelyn

I saw how upset Winnie was after Trixie was arguing, I stayed sitting down and remained silent. But then I saw Trixie look at me as Winnifred ran up to her room, I wanted to go and comfort her, but it wasn't my place. None of it was my place to say or do anything. And I wanted to be left out of it, but then Trixie and Winnie kept wanting me to choose sides. I didn't want to choose sides. I didn't think the rumble would end up causing strain on the whole family, given Winnie ran to the rumble behind my back, and behind Trixie's. I understand that Winnie did what she did and she shouldn't have I will admit it, but Trixie shouldn't have made the comment about mom and dad.

I could feel my hand shaking, I could feel my heart racing too. I didn't know why it was, maybe it was because I didn't think my sister's constant fighting, was not healthy for us. Especially when all of us are dealing with a rough patch.

"Same goes for you, Evelyn." Trixie said looking at me, "Keep going out with Dean, you'll get into trouble."

Why did she have to go after me? I was just minding my business.

"I asked you to leave me out of it Trixie," I said,

"Just saying you could've backed me up." Trixie snapped, "Your sister was in jail and you were just sitting here, probably going to sleep with Dean like one of his casual whores weren't you?"

"Goddamnit..." Evelyn said silently, "Leave him out of this, okay. He was at the rumble like you and Winnie were, and I went to go take care of Jenny when she left,"

"Did you know she went?" Trixie asked me angrily, "Did you know she was going to the rumble?"

"No!" I said, "Of course not. I kept telling her not to."

"Look, Evelyn I just really need you to cooperate with me, and honestly I am sick of this."

I just looked at her and was all upset. I definitely didn't want to get sent to a girl's home, I just hated being stuck in a tug of war between them and I didn't want to be forced to choose sides.

"You know what, not now. I can't." I said I didn't think I just went and ran off and left the house and ran away as far as I could. I didn't know where I was going to go, and I didn't know what I was thinking as I was running. But I had one place in my mind to hide for the night.

I didn't think I was going to end up there, but I did.

The Rebel Pony.

Because I was hoping that Dean would be there.

I snuck inside without an ID, hoping I could get in without getting noticed because I didn't want anyone to see me on the verge of sobbing, and I did. I saw Mark, the owner of the Rebel Pony, and tried to make sure he didn't see me because I was too upset to even look at anyone, but then I heard him call my name and I turned around.

"What are you doing here?" Mark asked me, he then saw me on the verge of tears, I tried to hold it in but it was too hard.

"Goddamn it Mark, if only you knew what life was like at home for me...Is Dean here?"

Mark nodded and went upstairs after he finished making someone's drink. I sat down on the couch where I usually sat. Then I saw two strange men staring at me, I was getting extremely uncomfortable and they started moving a little closer. But they clearly didn't get the hint that I wasn't interested and I felt uncomfortable around them. I then felt an arm go around me but it wasn't any of the strange men I turned around and saw that it was Dean. He hinted to the men to beat it and they did exactly that without hesitation.

"What's wrong, you?" He asked trying his best to be comforting when he actually wasn't doing so bad, I just didn't hold back my tears at this point from flowing down my face

"Can I crash for the night?"

"Of course," Dean responded, "Can you tell me what's bugging you?"

"My sisters got into this huge blowout fight. It was bad." I wept, I heard Dean sigh and he told me to go upstairs, I did that and followed his orders, he was more soft and sympathetic than he usually was, which was surprising to me. We reached upstairs and he brought me into his room and sat down and placed his hand on a seat next to him for me to sit. He was getting even more concerned by the second because I was just standing up and pacing back and forth, my hand my shaking and I was trying so hard to keep my family together, and trying my best to make sure nobody cracked, but I should've focused more on myself than anybody.

"Sit down." He said soft and sympathetic,

"I can't take it anymore, Dean!" I shouted as tears burst, "I have no one to go to. I can't tell Jo, I can't tell anyone. Only you. It's like I'm always stuck in the middle of everything. I'm trapped and I can't get out!"

I just looked down on the floor and started sobbing, I didn't want anyone to see me like this, let alone Dean. I found myself sinking into him more and more.

"Hey. Hey. Hey." He muttered cupping my face, "You're gonna be okay. I'm here."

Dean's voice was sounding softer and softer and let me rest the top of my head on his chin, something about that made me feel extremely safe.

"Goddamnit, why is life always this so goddamn frustrating." I wept as Dean continued to comfort me,

"It's gonna be okay." Dean claimed as he was rubbing my back to help me take a deep breath, "I hate seeing you like this."

For some reason, I started to feel myself getting flustered, which felt strange a bit especially since I was in my most vulnerable state, But I was also embarrassed because I heard him say that he "hated seeing me upset," only because he probably didn't want me to hear that, and I definitely knew that. And he knew I heard him.

"I'm sorry," I drawled, "I just didn't know where else to go."

"No need to apologize." Dean started to say trying to be comforting, "I understand. You can always come to me, Ev,"

I just nodded as I wiped the tears from my face, my face beat red from crying and Dean just smiled a bit, and I smiled too, I was already feeling a lot better. But I wasn't ready to go home yet, I couldn't face my sisters yet.

"Why are you being so nice to me?" I asked,

"First of all, I don't hate you. And second of all, you are my fake girlfriend anyway, I have to be nice." Dean answered, I snuggled into Dean and he smiled, but he thought I didn't see it, but I did. He wrapped his arm around me and I smiled.

"Why did you run to me?" He asked me.

But to be honest, I didn't know.

"You were the first person I thought of." I responded in an awkward tone, "And besides, we are a fake couple like you said, we might as well act like it."

"But Brian and Abi aren't here," Dean said,

"I know." I said, "But..."

"But what?" Dean asked and I just remained silent, I had so much I wanted to say but I couldn't let the words out of my mouth. Not yet. I didn't want to mess this up.

"I'm a little tired actually," I said, "I just want to sleep is that okay?"

"Of course," Dean answered smiling, he then got up and into his drawer and grabbed an old white t-shirt and threw it at me, "Here. If you want it. It's kinda old but it'll do. And whatever you do, don't be getting any ideas."

"Thank you," I said, "And I won't."

I went into the bathroom, to go and change and I took my floral dress and went into the T-shirt. It definitely smelled like Dean. It was old but it smelled like Dean. Then I overheard Dean, talking to Mark, who must have come in to ask what it was about. Dean didn't disclose that information which I appreciated because these were things that were all confidential between us. But then I heard him say a few things, that I wasn't really expecting him to say.

"Yeah, she's real sweet. Way better personality than Abigail that's for sure." I heard Dean say,

"She is," Mark said to Dean, "So, you have a crush on her?"

"No..." I heard Dean say, "Is it that obvious?"

"No, Jason told me." I heard Mark say,

"That rat."

I laughed as I heard Dean call Jason a rat, but then I was thinking I better get out of there soon before they think I'm dead or something. I got out of the bathroom and went into his room and Mark walked off.

"You kids be safe." Mark muttered walking out,

"You can have the couch over there. Here's a pillow." Dean said giving me a pillow, "Can I getcha anything else?"

"No, I'll be fine."

"You sure?"

"Yes."

"Of course." Dean said, "If you tell anyone about this you are dead."

"I don't plan on it, but...okay...." I said, "And thank you."

I went to the couch and started to rest my head. Dean started to take his shirt off and then go to turn off the light

"I get warm easily." Dean muttered and turned off the light in his room, "I said not to get any ideas."

Dean then went into his bed and I said "Goodnight,"

I had spent my time thinking if Dean actually was being true to what he was saying about me to Mark, I did trust Dean, I was really really starting to trust him, but I still needed to be careful because guys like Dean are only going to end up hurting me in the end and that was something I definitely needed to watch out for. I still couldn't sleep. I said I was tired but I couldn't sleep. I called Dean's name, who was clearly still wide awake, and he called for mine as well, almost mocking me in a way.

"Seriously, Ev what is it?" Dean asked,

"I can't sleep."

"What am I supposed to do about it?" He asked all snarky. He was still stubborn and in denial about things I heard him say. Typical of him.

"I don't know." I said, "I don't mean to be rude but Your room is...creepy."

"Oh, my bad, I didn't realize my decorating skills were that bad." He drawled in a sarcastic, witty tone. His attitude was definitely still there.

"A little sarcastic much?" I said,

"You find it attractive?" He asked

"Uh.... No..." I stuttered,

"Alright, I'll tell you what," Dean started to say, "What if I told you could come to sleep in my bed?"

"Are you sure?" I asked

"Do you want to be uncomfortable for the rest of the night?" He asked, "And possibly freeze your ass off? It's getting really cold. And I am warm and you get cold easily."

I shook my head and I crawled into bed with him, how did he know that I get cold really easily? That's what I was wondering. I must have mentioned it at one point. Dean was facing the opposite direction and then turned around.

"Better." He asked, I nodded.

But for some reason, I was still struggling to fall asleep. I tossed and turned for a bit hoping it would make a difference but it didn't. Dean turned around and noticed me tossing around so much. The first thing he asked me was "Are you okay?"

I nodded and just mentioned how I had a hard time sleeping lately, which was technically true. I did have a hard time sleeping. Especially with the way things have been.

"Ev," He whispered

"Hmm?"

I turned around and looked over and I saw him put his hand out for me to take it. I did exactly that and I smiled at him. That was sweet of him, it really was. I slowly then felt myself falling asleep.

The next morning, I woke up slowly, hearing a loud knocking on my door. And each moment it was getting louder and louder. The knocking woke up Dean and it got him incredibly annoyed.

"Mark, you know I like to sleep in on Saturdays..." Dean muttered as he started to get up and put his shirt on, He went over to the door and opened it, it wasn't Mark. It was Trixie.

"Oh it's you," Dean muttered annoyed, "what in The hell are you doing here?"

Trixie rolled her and eyes and just came in his room without warning.

"I came for Evelyn. I know she's here." Trixie stated

"She's not here." Dean lied, "You must be going crazy,"

I hide under the covers, hoping she wouldn't see me. But I had a feeling that wasn't going to help anything. Dean tried to shove her away but she refused to fight back.

"Don't fucking touch me! I'll beat the shit out of you so bad you won't even know what happened!" Trixie yelled, "you don't think I've dealt with low lives like you before? Uh? You don't. Go on say one more word. I dare you."

Dean just chuckled and I heard what sounded like a slap. I tried not to gasp so she wouldn't hear me.

"Now you better tell me where she is." trixie said, I felt something come even closer.

"I already told you, she isn't here. Now get outta my room." Dean claimed,

"I can see you Ev," I heard Trixie say as I slowly get out of the covers, "Should've known,"

I was getting more frustrated with her by the second.

"So you come here to solve your problems? How many times- Why- dammit Evelyn come here now! I am not asking again."

"Leave me alone Trixie" I shouted getting out of bed.

"So you've been up with Dean when we get into arguments?" Trixie asked, "Do you have any self-respect?"

"Hey, don't talk to her like that," Dean claimed,

"Look, I know you think Dean is some knight in shining armor, but he isn't." Trixie said,

"He's actually done more for me than you think." I said defending him.

"You know what? Go ahead and be with him, be with a criminal... I'm out." Trixie said storming off, and Dean wasn't going to let her get the last word in.

"And for the record," Dean said, I didn't think about what was coming out of his mouth next but his next few words hurt, "I'd never get with your sister..."

"Oh eat me Richards!" Trixie shouted from a distance. Dean shut the door, and I started to change into my normal clothes.

"I should go." I muttered.

"You're serious, you're gonna let Trixie get to you."

"It's not her, Dean." I said getting the rest of my belongings, "I can't believe that even for a second, we could've actually been real, and not just a trick to get back at richies."

"Hold it," Dean said taking my wrist and pulling me back, "What are you on about?"

I just blurted everything that I felt. I was nervous and upset all rolled into one, it was like he had a switch every time he was around certain people.

"I don't know, Dean. One moment to you I'm baby, and the next moment you say you want nothing to do with me? Which one is it? Because these past few months felt so real I started to believe it was however fake it was. And did me crying to you last night, does that mean anything to you? Because you seemed like you cared, you let me stay the night, in your bed for crying out loud. You wanna know what it means to me, is that I can trust you. And I hate being able to trust you. And after what you said to Trixie just now, I don't think I can go on with this any lon-"

Dean stopped my sentence and went in for a kiss. It felt like magic, and it felt like the butterflies in my stomach were finally being let go. I don't remember when a kiss actually felt this good. Dean stopped kissing me and he smiled, and then stopped his smile and muttered two words out of his mouth pointing to the door.

"Get out."

I was so confused, after what he had just did.

How could he?

"Evelyn, I'm serious." Dean said, "Get out of my face."

"After you just."

"Evelyn, go!"

I followed his orders and ran away in tears.

CHAPTER TWENTY-ONE

Trixie

After leaving the Rebel Pony, I felt my heart sink to my stomach.

I felt like I was failing my sisters.

I was getting more and more anxious thinking about it

I don't know where I went wrong with them.

Everything was going downhill and I felt it getting worse and worse by the minute.

I kicked a trash can as I was running away out of frustration and I was getting even more and more frustrated thinking about everything.

I grunted

I even hit a wall that was in front of me.

From Winnifred getting arrested to Evelyn falling for a criminal. And choosing to stay with Dean over her family???

What is wrong with her???

I was failing my sisters and I was failing myself. I didn't know what to do.

Should I have just given up?

Go back to college and just send the girls away?

Oh, then they would hate me forever.

Okay.

Calm down, Trixie.

Okay.

Just breathe.

Trixie.

Breathe.

It's alright now

Try not to think about everything all at once.

I went to the cemetery where my parents were buried, hoping I would get a glimpse of hope, hoping they could guide me through everything. But I didn't think they would hear me, because of course they were dead, and they weren't coming back. A part of me was still in denial about the fact that they were gone, and sometimes I forgot they existed in the first place because I ended up taking their places.

I kneeled down to their gravestones and I just started to speak from the heart. I felt myself almost about to break down. I looked and saw their graves.

Genevieve Martin

Beloved Mother, Wife, Sister

December 14th, 1915- May 21st, 1953

Gregory Martin

Beloved Father, Husband, Brother

June 12th, 1914 -May 21st 1953

I started to think about how their story started, they met in High School, when they were around Evelyn's age, he was an Idealistic and she was a Richie, and every night my mom used to sneak around just to see him, they fought against each other in a few rumbles, until their last rumble they fought together against the Richies. Evelyn always loved that story, she always loved the whole Star Crossed Lovers thing, and she also loved hearing it over and over again and it made her believe in love, it made her believe that Prince Charming was around her somewhere especially when she learned that they got married right after high school. It made her believe that Brian was a good guy, it made her believe in love and it made her believe that the rivalry could end if it could. But after Brian two-timed her, that only made the Rivalry worse, especially when girls like Valerie hear about things that the Richies have done. But then I started thinking about something. How Evelyn was just like mom. And I missed Mom so much.

"Mom, dad I let you down," I whispered, I felt myself shaking and on the verge of tears, but I did let them down entirely. But I just reminded myself that I am not a good parent and I have no clue what I'm doing, and I wasn't doing anything right. For all we knew it they were going to get sent away and be miserable. Winnie hates me and I can't protect Evelyn. I can't control them which means I can't keep them safe. I. I am young too.

"I just wanted to be a nurse, graduate from college. Make you proud. I can't sometimes. I don't want to lose the girls." I wept onto my parent's graves.

When I first started raising the girls, I thought all of this was going to be easy. But I was wrong. I was so wrong. I am not the most mature enough, I am not old enough or maybe I am just not good enough.

That's it.

That's what it is.

I'm not good enough.

I'm just a complete and utter failure.

"I need you guys. I'm scared, I'm tired." I said in between sobs, "Winnie ends up in jail. Evelyn is with a criminal. I just want you here with me."

I missed them like crazy, I needed them so much, I still needed so much to learn from them, and Winnifred and Evelyn needed them too.

"Please," I muttered softly and curled up in a ball next to their grave. "Please come back."

I took another deep breath and sighed. And I wanted them to know how much I appreciated all that they have done for me. I loved them and I missed them like crazy. I wanted them to be at my college graduation, my wedding, and the birth of my kids, there was so much more that I needed them for and I missed them so much. They weren't going to be there for Winnie and Evelyn's graduation and for their weddings either. I didn't know what I was going to do, I was never going to have my father give me away at my wedding, I was never going to have a father-daughter dance either, and my kids were never going to meet their grandparents. It all hurt too much thinking about it. And I was tearing up thinking about all of that. I slowly then started to feel myself falling asleep next to my parent's graves as I was crying so much.

I woke up hours later hearing my name being called which sounded like a mans voice, and I felt someone tapping my shoulder.

"Trixie..." the voice called out silently, I slowly started to wake up and I felt tears on my face. I looked up and saw that it was Max. What was he doing here?

"Did I fall asleep here?"

"Yeah, I've been trying to wake you for hours."

"Oh no!" I muttered,

"The cemetery doesn't seem like an ideal place for a nap," Max chuckled, "but maybe i'm mistaken."

"I like the Cemetery for a Nap." I joked, "It keeps me close with my parents."

Max looked and he saw who's grave I was at, and it all started to make sense to know why I was there in the first place. To feel closer to them and just have a conversation with them, even if they weren't going to answer me back.

"I come here a lot. To just talk to them, ya know?" I said,

"They must be proud of you, Trix." He said, I scoffed, I didn't know about that one.

"Proud? They would be anything but proud." I ranted to Max, "My sisters are in deep trouble. Both of them."

"You think they'd be in trouble?" Max asked, "Try having Valerie as your younger sister. He chuckled, in a way he was right, Valerie was causing more trouble than both of them.

"I guess,"

"You're doing your best. We all know it, and I'm sure your sisters do also." Max said, "And I think I am too. After my old man got arrested in Texas, I fleed Valerie here because I thought it was going to be best for her, but then I realized that she hadn't really changed one bit, but she's a seventeen-year-old girl struggling."

"I guess. Anyways, what brings you *here* on a walk?" I asked all curiously

"Only place I can get peace in this godforsaken town." Max claimed "As ironic as that sounds."

"Well, then I guess I should head back," Trixie said, "Maybe they finally will cool off."

"Can I walk you back?" Max offered,

"That would be great," I agreed, "Thank you."

CHAPTER TWENTY-TWO

Winnifred

The day after I got out of jail, Jenny and Valerie came to visit me, Jenny was happy to see me, while Valerie kept asking me a bunch of questions. She just couldn't believe that I was in jail.

"So, were the toilets gross?" Valerie asked,

"They were disgusting!" I claimed, "Grossest things I've ever seen."

"I can't believe you were in jail," Jenny said, "Was Trixie mad?"

I nodded.

"Who bailed ya out?" Val asked,

I didn't know if it was a good idea to tell her that it was Julia who bailed me out because I didn't know Valerie would feel about it, she definitely wouldn't believe me if I told her. So just told her the truth about Julia being the one that bailed me out. Valerie's jaw dropped when I told her, she couldn't really believe it. Val thought Julia was faking the nice act on us the entire time, and now she was starting to realize that Julia's nice act was real and she actually liked us.

"Wait... pause...." Valerie said still surprised, "One of the Richies....Bailed...YOU OUT?"

I nodded.

"Is that so hard to believe?" I asked,

"No." Jenny said

"Yes." Valerie said as Jenny said "No."

Jenny was extremely optimistic about it. She knew Julia and she knew how sweet she was. So she didn't think that Julia was fake in the slightest, while Valerie had spent the longest time not trusting her.

"That was very nice of her." Jenny said, "What happened after?"

"Then Trixie got mad and Evelyn ran away..." I added,

"Where did she go?" Valerie asked,

"Beats me,"

"What about Trixie?" Jenny asked,

"I'll be honest Jenny, I don't know and I don't care,"

I couldn't take any more questions about Trixie or me in jail. I mean I know I am going to end up in major trouble and I knew there was a high chance I got me and Evelyn sent away, but I was still really angry at Trixie she said I was going to end up like mom and dad, she then slut shamed Evelyn who had barely touched a guy, which really got me angry. Especially when Evelyn had finally cracked and it really upset me seeing Evelyn break down.

"Are you going to be sent away?" Jenny asked me, who was genuinely concerned about whether or not I was going to be get sent away. But the truth was I didn't know, I didn't know how much longer we were going to be in New York, and I didn't know where we were going to get sent to.

"I don't understand if you get arrested you get sent to a girl's home, meanwhile I've got arrested several times, and I'm still under Max's custody."

Jenny and I chuckled because we both knew she was right.

"I know, It doesn't make any sense," I said laughing, while Jenny clutched onto me,

"I don't want you to leave," Jenny said leaning on me, I started to think about Jenny and what would happen if I left, she wouldn't have anyone to run to her if she was struggling with her parents. Valerie was a good choice, but I was her go-to person, and what was she going to do without me. I didn't know.

Jo and Paulette came in minutes later.

"You little felon," Jo shouted.

"Hi." I muttered, "Good to see you too."

"How was jail?" Paulette asked,

"It was jail..." I said staring at Paulette and laughing, so much had been going in the past twenty-four hours, and I couldn't comprehend all of it. But that was life, and a lot was going to happen and we had to expect the unexpected most of the time.

"Where's Evelyn?" Jo asked, Valerie and I looked at each other and shrugged our shoulders.

"She ran off after me and Trixie's argument," I answered, "She seemed really upset, she didn't go to see you?"

Jo shook her head, and Paulette did the same thing, Valerie looked around and started to think.

"Do you think..." Valerie was about to state, "No, definitely not."

"What?" Jo asked,

"She could've gone with Dean," Valerie said, "I don't think that is the case but it could be."

"No, she wouldn't have," Paulette added,

"They've been spending A LOT of time together," Valerie added trying to sound smart, "Just saying, so you don't think that she went to him at his most vulnerable as a test to see if he maybe would... take care of her."

Jo looked at Valerie and was almost getting annoyed by her smart mouth, Paulette and I started to think about the fact that she could potentially be right, Evelyn was developing a crush on Dean, and she could've gone to see him to maybe see if he actually cared about her, but it was Dean, the only thing he cared about was himself, not another person, that was never the case with him.

"I'm just saying." Valerie sighed, "You guys are all dumb."

Jenny laughed and Jo started to roll her eyes, I could tell Jo was getting extremely annoyed with Valerie.

"Do you think I don't know my own best friend?" Jo asked, I looked over at Jenny and I knew this was not going to end quite well.

"I'm just saying you should pay attention to things once in a while." Valerie said arguing,

"Typical of you Valerie," Jo stood up, "You think you're better than me, you think you're better than all of us."

Valerie just sat down and chuckled, I could tell she didn't have the energy for anything, especially with fighting, since she had spent hours fighting people the night before and she knew she would win a fight, against literally anyone. Valerie looked at the ground so she didn't have to listen to a word that Jo was saying, and nothing got Jo annoyed more than being ignored.

"Ahem..." Jo coughed in her face, Valerie looked up,

"Yes Jo? May I help you?" Valerie asked, "Do you need a reality check?"

"Oooohhh." Paulette shouted, I whacked Paulette in the arm telling her to cut it out, and Paulette laughed,

"What is wrong with you?" Jo asked Valerie, "You just like to cause problems with everyone don't you?"

"Yes!" Val claimed, "Yes I do!"

"Don't you ever get exhausted?" Jo asked genuinely,

"No! Not really! I do love a fight!"

"Are you going to stop?"

"No!"

Jo was getting more frustrated I saw her clench her fists out of frustration. Valerie just chuckled sitting at her chair, waiting for Jo to do something.

"You're not fighting back because you know I can beat your ass." Valerie claimed, "So you don't even bother."

"You know, I really want to kill you sometimes!" Jo shouted, those were the words that got Jenny scared, she clutched onto me like a little kid who wanted to stay with her mother, I wrapped my arm around her and whispered to her that it was okay, and they needed to grow.

I looked at the two of them, and encouraged them to stop because they were upsetting Jenny. Valerie looked at me and Jenny and I whispered "Stop" to Valerie and looked at Jo and did the same thing. Val looked over and Jenny and she stopped, while Jo sat down and stopped.

"I'm sorry Jenny," Valerie said, "I don't mean to act like this,"

"Look at you actually having compassion for another person." Jo claimed while clapping, "Round of applause for you Valerie Darling! You're finally not being the selfish accident that you are."

That was the straw for Valerie, and she got up and shoved Jo. I was getting upset and I got Jenny out of the room as they were fighting. I brought Jenny in the other room so she didn't get scared. I heard a loud grunt from someone from the other room, and I told Jenny I was going to see what it was about and told her I would be right back. I went back in the room and saw that Jo and Valerie were actually fighting. And I looked at Paulette and saw that she was trying to break it up, I pulled Valerie away while Paulette pulled Jo away.

"YOU TWO ARE RIDICULOUS!" Paulette shouted,

"You're acting like complete and utter animals, are you guys insane?" I asked, "Poor Jenny is crying in the bathroom right now and you are seriously arguing over who knows Evelyn better, are you serious right now?"

"Yeah, seriously, shouldn't her safety matter first?" Paulette asked and I nodded agreeing with her.

"Yes." Jo and Val said in unison sounding a little monotone.

"Now..." I said then I heard a slamming door coming from the front, it was definitely either Trixie or Evelyn.

The door opened and I saw that it was Evelyn.

CHAPTER TWENTY-THREE

Evelyn

I went inside and I just kept muttering under my breath.

I can't believe how stupid I was.

what an asshole.

Guys are so confusing.

And I poured my fucking heart out! I was starting to open up after he tells Trixie that he'd never get with me, and kissed me, out of the blue.

And then I get told to get out?

I mean... What the actual hell?

What kind of person does that to another?

I went into my room and saw Winnie, Val, Jo, and Paulette all together, they all stared at me and saw me upset.

"What's wrong with you?" Valerie asked me,

"Dean... I went to see Dean. Okay? After my fight with Winnie and Trixie, I went to the rebel pony." I answered honestly,

"I TOLD YOU!" Valerie shouted and then stared at everyone as they were all telling her to read the room, "I mean...why were you with Dean?"

"Just stop asking questions." I said, "I'm already upset enough,"

"No. No. No. Ev, what is going on?" Jo asked, "What did he do?"

"What do you wanna know?" I asked trying to hold back my tears, "You wanna know that Dean and I kissed ten minutes ago!?"

Everyone's jaws were wide open, fully out of surprise, especially Jo and Valerie who were staring at each other.

"I knew it, I knew it! I told you Jo, didn't I?" Valerie asked looking at Paulette,

"Holy cow!" Paulette claimed, "You were right Val,"

"Both of you, shut your traps." Jo said to Paulette and Valerie "And you what?"

I answered the question again, "We kissed! Me and Dean..."

"We heard you the first time Evelyn," Winnie said, Jo and Winnie had the same reaction, while Val and Paulette clearly guessed it from the beginning,

"Why are you so upset if you just kissed Dean Richards?" Paulette asked me trying her best to comfort me, I sighed, I didn't understand why it was so hard to say. But it was the truth, if Trixie was here, I would have gotten a big fat "Told you so" from her. But Trixie wasn't here, and luckily my friends were here to comfort me and not just say 'Told you so'

"So why were his lips on yours?!" Valerie asked, "I want to know what made him go all jackass on you,"

"Don't ask me, ask him." I claimed and was feeling completely and emotionally drained, "I'm just so confused, and I'm so stupid for even thinking he can change."

"Well, here is what is going to happen," Valerie said, "Jo and I are going to have a little chat with that man whore,"

"Uhhh... Val...is that a good idea?" Winnifred asked,

"Yes, he's scared of me, he knows what I can do to him, so yeah,"

Valerie then marched off with Jo, and Paulette followed them and I stayed with her, and I completely forgot that Jenny was still in the bathroom, she came outside of the bathroom and noticed that I was home, and asked Winnie why I was upset. Winnifred just told Jenny to never trust men, because they are all just complete rats. And that was true, they were confusing rats that was for sure.

"I mean it's not fair." I said "Why do you guys just make me feel like shit when I pour my heart out. I fall for the ones that don't deserve me. Or what am I doing wrong?"

"I don't know," Jenny said, "You're a good person Evelyn, and Dean is just not thinking straight."

"Dean is so confusing... and I stayed the night" I revealed, "... in his bed..."

"Wait what?" Jenny said surprised

"Scandalous." Winnie added,

"In his bed... and that's rare for most girls."

"You're right, it is." Winnie said, "Unless you did the deed."

I shook my head and mentioned that it didn't happen.

"We didn't..." I mentioned, "it was actually nice."

"Whoa, that is rare..." Winnie said and I couldn't tell if she was mocking me or not with her tone, "How bout this... go get some rest, I'm sure Dean will come around..."

I did exactly that and just went into the other room to take a quick little nap.

Hours later, I woke up to someone calling my name and shaking me constantly, it was a girls voice, I woke up slowly and saw that it was Winnifred. Winnifred shook me again until I finally was wide awake.

"What is it?" I asked, "Why did you wake me?"

"Ummm someone's out the window," Winnifred pointed over to the window and I saw Dean waiting out of the window, Dean waved at me and I walked over to him,

"Let me in," He muttered,

"Why should I?" I was clearly emotionally drained, and I didn't want to see anyone. Especially Dean.

"Please... I need to explain myself...Please...." Dean begged,

"Fine." I let Dean in and he finally got into my room, he fell to the ground and then got right back up again

"Ok, I'm just gonna go downstairs so if you two are gonna do anything, just don't go in my bed okay. Thank you..." Winnie said tip-toeing away and stared at her as she walked off. I was already emotionally drained and tired.

"Do you have a moment?" Dean asked,

"What is it?"

"Listen Evelyn, I didn't wanna make you cry. That was the last thing I wanted to do." Dean sighed,

"The why did you huh?" I asked, "Because you say you didn't want to make me cry and that's exactly what you did. So why did you?"

"Look. I'm an asshole. I know that." Dean agreed with himself, "And I Know It's not gonna change. But I'm trying, I just... I just don't know what to do. Tell me what to do."

I sighed and I was feeling a little bit calmer now, but it seemed to me that Dean was truly trying to be better.

"You can't get away with things with just apologizing and then just expect me to move on. You are just- just so-complicated."

"I know. Okay? But like I said I'm trying right now, you gotta realize, it's different baby. It's different with you. I just feel like when I'm around you, there's this side of me I never thought I'd ever see. And trust me it's a damn good side. And Honestly, starting this trick was worth it because it got to be close... to you. And man, I kissed you, and man it was one of the best kisses of my life. I mean I didn't even think it could be like that, a kiss like that, and I regret telling you to get out. Because trust me, Evelyn, that was the last thing I wanted to do, and I'm glad I kissed you okay. I wanted to kiss you. I wanted to do it for a while babe. It's just... I..."

He then leaned in and cupped my face, I didn't know what he was going to do, was he going to kiss me? Or something else

"I care about you okay," Dean added

"I... I don't know what to say." I sighed,

"Don't say anything," Dean said,

"But..." I said, "You're sitting here in front of me, vulnerable and apologetic, this is not like Dean Richards I know. What is going to happen next?"

"To be honest," Dean said, "I have no damn clue."

I just laughed and Dean laughed too, this was nothing like Dean, and I was wondering what I have done to deserve this, and Dean was wondering what he did to deserve me.

"Don’t tell anyone about this, Ev. A girl like you has no business with a guy like me. You know that." Dean smiled, deep down I always knew that Dean was a good guy. And he wasn't terrible and a monster like most people thought he was. He was just a boy who had been hurt too many times.

"You have a business to be with anyone you want," I said, "Even if it's a nervous wreck like me."

I looked over and I saw that Dean was blushing a bit. I noticed it, and decided to say something, he protested and said that he wasn't. I teased him about it tremendously and said that he was blushing, and he just kept blushing, even more than before when I called him out, it was noticeable too.

"Do you think we'll ever be real and not just a trick?" I asked,

"If I'm honest," Dean started, I was getting a little bit nervous to hear what he was going to say, I didn't know if he was going to say no.

But then I heard the words, "I would like that,"

I started grinning like a child seeing candy at the candy shop. And he did the exact same thing, I never imagined anything more perfect, mainly because I never expected it.

I guess this is what it was supposed to feel like.

"Can I come by later?" Dean asked, I nodded and he walked over to me and kissed my cheek. Dean then climbed out from the window and I looked out the window.

"Dean you are crazy." I muttered.

CHAPTER TWENTY-FOUR

Trixie

As Max walked me back to my house, we spent some time talking, and then we finally reached our destination, I smiled at him and he smiled back at me.

"Thanks for walking me home Max," I said gratefully, "And thank you for speaking with me,"

"Anytime, I know you're doing your best, and I see it."

"Thank you, finally someone sees it," I said, and I hugged Max, I finally felt like I was being appreciated or that I was finally doing something right. I just hoped that the girls were going to be alright in regards to whether or not they were going to be sent to a girl's home. I got back inside the house and saw nobody in the kitchen, I called for the girls, hoping I would hear an answer, but there was no response. Both the girls were mad at me and I knew that. And I didn't think they were going to forgive me. I went too far. I sat down at the kitchen table and I spent time thinking, thinking about everything, everything that went down in the past twenty-four hours.

Hours later, I heard the sounds of a door-knocking repeatedly, I kept calling for the person to come in and kept telling them it was unlocked, I was only getting annoyed with the constant knocking because I first thought it was Valerie, Jo, or Paulette.

"It's unlocked." I said as the door continued to knock, "It's Unlocked, you can just come in."

But then I was getting more annoyed by how loud and obnoxious the knocking sound was, and I finally went to open the door. And saw a familiar face, Ms. MacaFee, the social worker.

"Oh, hello Ms. MacaFee, good to see you," I said, "I'm sorry if I sounded rude earlier, I thought you were one of my sister's friends."

"May I come in?" Ms. MacaFee asked,

"Yes of course, Please." I said welcoming Ms. Macafee in the house I felt nerves coming into my system especially when Ms. MacaFee was in the house hours after everything was happening, I knew that she knew about Winnie's arrest, "Sorry for the mess and Sorry I'm dressed in these clothes. You can sit down if you would like."

Ms. Macafee sat down, and it was silent for a couple of seconds, I was getting more and more nervous and I did some sucking up to her as I was feeling the tensity and the anxiety running in my veins.

"Can I get you a glass of water or something?" I asked

"No thank you." She responded,

"I'm sorry to ask this. I mean no disrespect but why are you here?" I asked her even more and more nervous, I didn't know why I asked her, because deep down, I knew exactly what it was about.

"word is going around the office about Winnie's record lately." She responded, I took a large gulp and I felt my heart sink to my stomach, I knew that this wasn't going to be good.

"It was a misunderstanding." I said doing my best to defend Winnie's actions, "I have already-"

She interrupted me by telling words that I wished to not here from her, but it was going to happen given our status. I already was in tears, and I couldn't take it.

"I'm sorry but they made the decision to-" Ms. Macafee said all sympathetic,

"No...They haven't gotten into trouble before. This isn't them." I said,

"The Court and I did have a little discussion, about it, and we were thinking there can be a custody court case for why you should keep your sisters."

"When is this going to be?"

"Next week,"

I had one week to prove that I can take care of my sisters, One week to show that I was a fit enough guardian to look after the girls. I didn't know how I was going to do it. But I knew I could do it. But I was having loads and loads of doubts.

"Thank you Ms. Macafee," I said, "I'll see you next week."

"You're welcome,"

"I promise, I won't let you down."

Ms. Macafee smiled and gave me a hug. As she left and I sighed sitting down onto the chair, trying to not burst into tears but it was of joy and fear rolled into one, but I also was bursting into laughter. Thinking about the thought of how this could end up either good or bad. I didn't know what they all thought of me, and people I knew were most likely going to testify. I didn't want any of the

Richies to testify either, I just didn't want to have to deal with them saying things about me.

Winnifred came in and smiled awkwardly, and I looked over at her.

"Who was at the door?" She asked, I didn't say a word, until she asked me again, "Trix, who was it?"

"Social Services." I answered angrily, I stood up and I was getting more upset, "So you guys might be getting sent to a girls home, and that is on you Winnie because you were so stupid you chose to go to that goddamn rumble and get yourself arrested."

"Goddamnit," Winnie said, "You think I don't feel bad enough for it."

I immediately placed my hands on my face out of frustration. I sighed and I looked over at Winnie who was clearly upset enough.

"I'm sorry Winnie, I don't mean to take it out on you," I said, "And I'm sorry for everything that I said,"

"I know you are Trixie." Winnifred said accepting my apology, "I know you are,"

Evelyn came in just a couple of minutes later from upstairs and I looked over at her,

"There you are, we've been looking everywhere for you,"

Evelyn smiled and walked over to me and hugged me. She hugged me as tight as she possibly could, it was clear that she felt bad for everything that had happened.

"I'm so sorry Trixie," she responded, "I'm sorry I lost it, I was just stressed."

"I know you were hun." I said, "I know. I'm not mad. I'm sorry I got mad at you for who you wanted to hang out with. It wasn't my place to judge you."

"If anything I should have been listening to you," Evelyn answered,

"You know social services came today," Winnie said,

"What?" Evelyn asked, "When?"

"Just now, they have been thinking about sending you guys to a girl's home, we are going to have a court case for it soon." I told Evelyn,

"So we might have to leave you? Leave everyone?"

I nodded and looked at the girls, and reminded them not to worry, because I was going to figure it out, I always found a way to figure it out.

Because there was nothing I wouldn't do for Winnie and Evelyn.

CHAPTER TWENTY-FIVE

Winnifred

I didn't think that Social Services would end up coming to our house, and it was my fault. Maybe Trixie was right, it was my fault.

Now because of me, I could be getting sent to a girl's home.

And Evelyn too.

I didn't want to leave.

But now we might have to.

It's my fault.

Only I wasn't so goddamn stubborn.

I have the life here that I love and I enjoy, I have friends here that are almost like family. Jenny, she needed me, and she wasn't going to have me. Valerie would need someone to keep her and Jenny in line and I didn't know how she was going to be calmer without me around. But Valerie needed me, Jenny needed me, and if I got sent to a girls home I wouldn't know what to do if they weren't there.

But I had to act fast, before it was too late. I had to make amends with everyone, everyone in my family.

They all needed me to be hero.

But I didn't know how I was going to do that, especially when everyone was probably mad at me. Even Trixie, I knew she meant no harm by lashing out at me, but she had every right. I was the reason Social Services came in the first place.

I spent the entire night thinking about what I was going to do next, I barely got any sleep thinking. I was in tears most of the night in my bed, because I didn't know what I was going to do in regards to everything. I sobbed as hard as I could, but I remembered that crying was not going to solve anything.

I turned around and saw that Evelyn was right behind me, when I had tears fully streaming, I didn't want to show her that I was sad, but she already knew, she knew I had been crying for a while.

"Are you still upset about the social worker?" Evelyn asked me,

"Of course I am, given the fact that I am the reason it happened in the first place. But there's nothing we can do."

"You're right, there is nothing we can do." Evelyn said, "But we can always figure it out as we see where the trial goes."

"How long is it going to take?"

"I don't know."

"I need to go." I said, going outside, but I just needed fresh air, to think. Think about everything that was happening, I was mad at myself more than I ever could be and I was causing enough damage and my family was no where near happy. As I went on my walk, I saw that the Richies were driving near me, I ran away as fast as I could because I didn't need anything to deal with, especially the Richies. I ran far away, far away from the Richies, and then I hid, I hid from them and ended in a small alley, as I was running off I bumped into a familiar face, Stephanie Dawn. Which was someone I haven't seen since the rumble. And she was someone I felt a bit intimidated by, she was very similar to Valerie, only she was more reckless and tough and violent.

"You're Evelyn's sister aren't you?" Stephanie asked me,

"Yeah,"

"Winnie? Right?'

I nodded.

"You shouldn't be in this side of town," Steph said, "This is where it's a little rough."

"I know, I was running away from the Richies because they were speeding through to come after me."

"Oh... so... I'm actually glad I ran into you, I want to talk to you." Steph started to say as she sat down against the wall. I sat down next to her and she offered me a cigarette. I kindly turned it down.

"So Dean's in love with your sister, did you know that?"

"Yes I did, who didn't." I responded, "Is that what you want to talk to me about, Evelyn and Dean,"

"No. That's not it, I wanted to talk to you about you getting arrested." Stephanie started, 'first of all you're the smartest out of all of us, Advanced Classes, with a 3.9 GPA, how the hell did you get caught by the goddamn cops?"

"You know I don't know," I responded as she basically tore into me. I just couldn't help but laugh. Because Stephanie was right, how did I end up getting caught, "I guess I just got freaked out and I froze."

Stephanie chuckled. She then looked at me sternly, she couldn't believe how I got arrested still. But sometimes there were things that I couldn't expect from myself.

"After that happened, social services came to our house," I told stephanie, "And now Evelyn and I might be sent to some girls home,"

"Oh Damn," Stephanie said, "Does Evelyn know?"

"Of course she knows," I said, "She was there."

Stephanie looked at me, and she started to laugh, I laughed along with her, I don't know why I did, but something about her was something I kind of admired, she was sure of herself and she did things without caring about the consequences. She also hung out with the worst of the worst influences, which was one of the reasons why she didn't care, she committed loads of crimes in this town, and she drank all day, fought people without caring about if they go thurt or even died, she did what she did.

Stephanie finished her cigarette and I watched as she threw it on the ground, She noticed how I was staring at her and she looked over.

"So, how's Valerie? Still a bitch?" Steph asked,

"I mean, she's always been like that, but we love her." I added,

Steph chuckled and looked at me again. And asked me a question in regards to my situation.

"So if you want, I can testify...for all of you guys,"

"What?"

"Why not?" She started, "I can get Dean, but I can't have Jason, our other friend because he is a complete idiot, but Dean is smart, and I know he'd do anything I say."

"So you would help us?" I asked her,

"Why not?"

CHAPTER TWENTY-SIX

Evelyn

I didn't know how to help Winnie, who was getting more and more upset by the minute. And we were getting sent away, and I couldn't let that happen, things were starting to go alright between me and Dean. And he started to see me for who I was, I needed to see him, I needed to see him and let him know what was happening. But I was wondering how he was going to react, especially with how everything was going. I told Trixie that I needed to head out, and as I walked to the door.

"Hey Trix, I'm gonna head out," I said walking out,

"Okay, be back for dinner," Trixie said, "I'm making Lasagna,"

"Alright. Okay." I said, I walked out of the house and slammed the door, and walked out of the house and got to the alley, the same alley that's on the way to the Rebel Pony. I walked to the door of the Rebel Pony and was about to knock until Mark, the bar owner opened the door.

"You again, Jesus Christ." Mark claimed,

"Is Dean here? I'll only be a minute." I asked, "Please, it's urgent,"

Mark shut the door and I got angry, I didn't appreciate his rudeness. But I was hoping he would let me in, as the door opened several minutes later, Dean went to get the door and he was almost stunned to see me his dark eyes widened.

"Hey you." Dean smiled, "What are you doing here?"

"Do you have a moment, outside please?" I asked him, Dean nodded and went outside to sit next to me at the edge of the wall.

"What's going on kid?" Dean asked,

"I..." I couldn't think, I didn't know how to word all of it, "I might be leaving..."

"What? What do you mean?" Dean started to cup his face, "Leaving where?"

"Social services came by after Winnie got arrested so that means I might be going to a girl's home."

"What the hell?" Dean asked, "What the hell did you do?"

"Absolutely nothing." I said, "Social Workers are putting us through court to see if our sister is stable enough to be our guardian, and if not, we get sent to the Girl's home, and it's pretty far."

"I'm sorry Ev, is there anything you need from me?" Dean asked, and I couldn't believe it, Dean wanted to help, and of course I was beyond grateful by him wanting to help me but there really wasn't much for him to do, especially since there was nothing that was in his control, it was all legal things, and social workers.

"I really wish you could," I said, "But you can testify."

"And say what, that Trixie slapped me in the face?" Dean laughed, "Even though I deserved it since I was kind of being a prick."

"You were being a prick." I said,

"Wow..."

"I'm sorry..."

"I've never heard you curse before."

"Now you have," I said laughing.

Dean looked at me and his laughter lasted for a while until moments later things started to get quiet. Dean was silent, and it looked like he had something he wanted to say.

"I don't want you to leave Ev," Dean said

"I don't want to leave either..." I said, "But I don't know what's going to happen now,"

Dean then took my hand and reminded me that everything was going to be fine, and he meant what he said when he said he cared about me a lot. Dean then leaned in and kissed my cheek, and did nothing for a little bit. I wasn't going to let him get away this easily, as I leaned in and kissed his lips, it felt like heaven. I didn't think I was going to fall for the town's biggest criminal and let alone I didn't think he would fall for me. As he let go, he apologized and I didn't know why

"You don't have to stop." Evelyn said,

"I know. I don't want to ruin it."

"You couldn't ruin it,"

Dean smiled as he heard those words come out from my mouth. He was pleased to hear that I cared about him the same way he cared about me. All I wanted was for him to know that I cared, and he cared about me too. Which was something that I still was in disbelief about.

I kissed Dean again on the lips for a second, and Dean smiled and kissed me again.

"So," Dean started to say, he had a lot on his mind in regards to what was going to happen, "How can I help?"

"Just be honest," I said, "You're the most honest person I know."

Dean smiled and looked at me, I didn't know how honest he was going to be in regards to the court trial, But he was helping me so I didn't know what was going to go wrong.

CHAPTER TWENTY-SEVEN

Trixie

The day of the trial occurred, and I got dressed up, especially for the occasion, I didn't have many dress clothes, so I looked and saw that my mom had some old clothes. I found her jacket and a button shirt with pants that could work to make me look professional, I came downstairs, and saw that Winnifred and Evelyn were waiting for me. They were all dressed up as well.

As I went outside the girls followed me and I drove them to the Courthouse. As soon as we got there, I stopped the car and turned around to look at the girls. I saw the distress on Winnie and I saw Evelyn was trying her best to comfort her and made sure that she knew that everything was going to be fine. But we all knew that everything wasn't going to be fine. We didn't know what was going to happen, our fate, my fate with the girls was no longer in my hands. It was all on the law at this point.

As we sat down in the aisles, I looked over and turned around to see Valerie and Max were across from me, I waved at them and Valerie and Max waved back. I looked over to see that Dean was sitting next to Evelyn

"What are you doing here?" I asked him,

"I'm here in support for Evelyn, and the rest of you," Dean said sternly, "I know you don't trust me but I am here for the support."

"Thank you Dean." I heard Winnifred say, I turned around and looked at her, I didn't know if Winnie was for or against Dean being here. But I knew Evelyn was happy to see him especially when I saw the smile on her face when she saw him. I wanted to smack it off her.

"All rise." I hear the judge say as I look at Winnie and Evelyn, "We are here for a family matter. Of deciding on the custody of Winnifred and Evelyn Martin, deciding if they belong in the custody of their older sister, Beatrice Martin. How old are the girls Beatrice?"

"Fourteen and sixteen your honor," I said looking at them and Winnie smiling,

"You are about to turn twenty two next september?"

"September 3rd your honor," I said, My Birthday is September 3rd, 1932."

"And when are your sister's birthdates?"

"Winnifred is January 11, 1939, and Evelyn is March 1, 1937."

I looked over at my sisters. And I felt sweat dripping down my face and looked at everyone else that was in the courthouse.

"My first witness is Maximus Darling. Max Darling please rise."

Max gets up and stands at the witness stand.

"How well do you know the Martin girls Mr. Darling?"

"I've known Ms. Martin since high school, your honor?" Max said, "And I happened to become great friends with her ever since, we bonded over raising our younger siblings."

The judge looked at Max, who then looked at me, I was thinking too much. Thinking a lot about how the judge was going to react to all of this. Because he was deciding my and my sister's fates at the end of the day. I looked over and saw that Dean was holding Evelyn's hand as the judge continued to question Max, I wasn't paying attention to what the judge was asking and I wasn't paying much attention to what Max was saying answering, because I had all of these thoughts going through my head and I didn't what was going to happen next.

The Next Witness, was someone I hoped I would never have to see again, but he lived in the town and was very famous in this town. It was Brian Scott.   I looked over and saw Evelyn getting nervous, and saw Dean clenching his fists together so he didn't get violent with Brian right then and there. As Brian sat on the witness stand, I looked at Dean and tried to take a deep breath.

"State your name and relation to the family Mr. Scott." I hear the judge say,

"Brian Scott, your honor and I'm the former boyfriend of the middle daughter Evelyn," Brian said,

"How did things end between the two of you,"

I saw Brian look at me, and stare me down, and I saw him look at Dean, and I watched as Dean was trying not to get violent, I stared at Dean and reminded him not to.

"Because of her psychotic older sister" Brian said, we all knew he was lying. I knew, Dean knew and Evelyn knew. That Brian was a compulsive, pathological liar, and we were not going to let him get away with this.

"What sort of things would she do?"

"Threaten me to leave if I didn't walk out, you see she didn't like the thought of a rich guy being with her poor, sad, depressed baby sister, who is too stupid to realize that no one else would have her..."

"Objection!" Dean shouted,

"You can't shout objection Richards," Brian stated, "You're not a goddamn attorney."

"I am...going to literally strangle him..." Dean said to Evelyn,

"We are not strangling anyone, other wise you'll end up getting into trouble, and I don't want that." Evelyn said to him, I looked at Evelyn and asked if she was alright, she said she was.

"Your honor may I say a few words." Dean stood up,

"Dean. NO!" I claimed,

"Dean Richards, good to see you again." Judge claimed,

"I'm sorry why is the criminal talking..." Brian claimed, Dean interrupted him and added a comment to him. It was all to make sure everyone knew who Brian Scott, the mayor's son really was.

"You know Brian," Dean said, "Lying under oath is a criminal offense, you know how things really ended between you and Ev,"

"Dean..." I said, "I don't want you getting in trouble, and not for me, not for Evelyn, I'm begging you."

Dean looked at me and stared at Evelyn, and I didn't know what he had up his sleeve, but Dean was willing to lie for me, and for my sisters.

"I think Trixie is an incredible guardian." Dean said, "Over the past few months, I started to get to know her, and she is one of the bravest, protective, strongest women I know, she is giving and she is always looking out for her sisters, and will always do anything to protect them. Even when I felt as if I was falling in love with her sister, and Trixie had to second guess me because of my past. But I know she did it to protect her, I know she would kill for Evelyn, and I know she would kill for Winnie, and this is about Winnie, I know and she is a really bright kid, a big future ahead of her, and all she did was want to help us. So please... give them a chance to stay..."

"Silence," The judge said, "This is no rash action matter, Richards, given your history of being in court we will not be calling you the witness stand."

"This is nonsense." Dean said, "This is bullshit man."

Dean sat down and huffed, Evelyn took his hand out of comfort, I looked over and was wondering if Dean meant what he was saying.

I just didn't need any more stress, and my sisters deserved the world, and more. And I don't know if they would ever survive a girls home, and especially being in isolation.

CHAPTER TWENTY-EIGHT

Winnifred

I watched as Trixie was getting distressed in the courtroom, more sweat was dripping down her face and I couldn't do anything to help her. I just wanted to rush to her aid and apologize for everything I caused. I couldn't help but express my guilt.

When the judge called for a recess, I felt myself shaking. I looked over at Evelyn, and I was having all of those thoughts in my head, about how I was the problem, not Trixie. And if they were going to send us to a girl's home it should be just me and not Evelyn. I still didn't understand why Evelyn was getting punished for my actions. I was sorry... I was really sorry. It took everything in me to not start crying right then and there.

After the recess, all of us walked into the courtroom and me and my sisters held hands. There was another person called to the Witness stand, someone who I didn't expect to be called. Julia Rose. I didn't think she was going to testify, especially for me. But I should've also known, she was on our side more than The Richies and she always was on our side more than theirs. I looked at her and I waved at her, then I mouthed "thank you" I was definitely happy that she was there, but I didn't know what she was going to say, which had me nervous.

"How do you know the Martin Girls?"

"I go to school with them Your Honor, and I helped the Youngest Ms. Winnifred Martin with her studies, and sometimes she helped me."

"Were you at the fight where Winnifred was arrested?"

"No Your Honor, but I did bail her out because Ms. Martin couldn't afford it."

"How can she support her sisters, if she can't clean up their messes..." I turned around as I heard Brian mutter those words, I wanted to flip him the bird, but it was definitely not the right time for me to do so. Especially when there was a judge right there.

"Well, I was always friends with her youngest sister, and helped her through some of her toughest times, like when she was having issues with some of my former friends, or if they were harassing her."

I turned around and saw that Paulette and Jo were behind me, I didn't even notice until just recently. Jo took my hand in support and we both watched as Julia was saying how our living status was, she didn't say much that was good, but she didn't say much that was bad either. So that was when I was really starting to get worried, given the circumstances. I didn't see anything good coming out of this.

"Order." I hear the judge say, I missed the rest of Julia's statement...

OH DEAR.

This is going to be bad. Really. Really bad.

That was all I was thinking in that moment. I just didn't know what was going to happen next. Nobody knew what was happening next, I certainly didn't know. None of it was in our control anymore. It was all everyone else.

And what the town thought of us, because not everyone liked us, and I knew that. They thought of me as a Know it all most of the time, they thought that Evelyn was too scared and too meek most of the time, and Trixie was seen to be a hothead who lost herself after losing her parents. But she did lose herself, we all did, myself and Evelyn, and sometimes us losing ourselves could end up resulting in these kinds of things.

And most importantly Brian's father was there, the mayor. Mayor Scott, who all of us Idealistics really hated. Myself included.

His father practically owned the city so when he got called to talk, all he mentioned was how his son knew Evelyn and Trixie for being psychotic, which I knew wasn't true, and that only made me even angrier and angrier not just the mayor, but at the town.

Because no one was listening to our side.

CHAPTER TWENTY-NINE

Evelyn

I spent most of the trial fixated on Dean, hoping I could get a little bit of comfort from him. And he was doing a good job at helping. I looked over and then saw that Jason and Stephanie walk in and a judge called for Stephanie Dawn to the witness stand, Stephanie, Stephanie Dawn as in Dean's friend, who didn't really like me but then forgot about her jealousy and gave me excellent advice in regards to Dean. I didn't think she was going to testify and help me in this situation. But she did. She did try and help me which was something I didn't expect to happen.

"How do you know the Martin girls?" the judge asked Evelyn

"I go to school with them your honor," Stephanie answered rightfully and honestly, "I didn't really know them both, but I judged them immediately before I got to know them, especially Evelyn, I thought she was this prude, but she's really sweet."

I couldn't believe what was happening, Stephanie Dawn, who hated me when I and Dean started, was saying all of these nice things, about me. I didn't see any of it coming. I looked over at Dean and he was equally as surprised as I was.

"And why did you judge her? Was it because of her family life?"

"No, It was because I was jealous of her, I was jealous because she was taking my best friend away from me, and taking him for herself." Stephanie added, "And she's honestly just a girl that had been hurt too many times, and she's nowhere near one of those girls that people judge her for, and looking at her sisters, I think her sister is doing a good job, and I barely even know her."

I looked at Stephanie and saw that she was looking at me, I couldn't believe it. Stephanie smiled over at me and then she smiled over at Dean. I didn't think she was going to try and help especially when our interactions weren't always the most pleasant, like when I first came to the Rebel Pony, she just went after me and attacked me, but then when I confided in her about Dean, she helped me do something about it.

But this was different, it was completely different from the regular teenager things that were used to, this was different than Brian Scott and his friends being sexist towards us and the rest of the Idealistic girls, this was the real stuff, and if no one liked me now, who knew if they were going to like me when all of this was over, or were they going to continue their hostile behavior towards us. I didn't know, but I was hoping that Stephanie was going to be better towards me, because after all, she did get a change of heart.

"Did you ever happen to think of her family as unstable Miss Dawn?"

"No your honor, I just saw them as having to go through a difficult time in their lives."

"Did you ever find them as difficult to be around?"

"No, not particularly, I don't really know the older one, but I've gotten to know the younger two pretty okay, and they seem alright." Stephanie smiled

"Thank you." The judge said, "We will come to a decision after the recess."

As we all went outside the courtroom, I looked over for Stephanie and saw her and walked over to her. I didn't know what was about to come out of my mouth but I just needed to get all the right words in so I didn't get myself into trouble with her, she was just growing to like me, and the same way around. I didn't want to mess that up. And I was also going out with her best friend. So that was another thing I needed to think about, I wanted her to like me because her and Dean were good friends, but it wasn't going to be easy.

"I guess a thank you is in order," I said to her

"Yeah anytime," Steph said, "I did what I could to help,"

"And you did, why?"

"I ran into your sister and she was definitely distressed and I wanted to help, I've seen people be separated from their families and it is not something people look forward to." Stephanie started to say, "And what happened at the Rumble wasn't really your sister's fault, it wasn't Trix's either, people just were selfish and they wanted one person to take the fall for it."

I didn't know what was going to happen next and I was terrified of what was occurring, I looked over to Stephanie and just hugged her, I was grateful for all that she was doing, even if it wasn't much. It was more than enough. Steph and I let go of each other and Dean came up from behind Stephanie and both of us looked at him and laughed.

"You two bury the hatchet?" Dean asked,

"Yeah, she's alright now I guess."Steph started to say, "You starting to like her now,"

"Yeah I am," Dean responded and we both saw his face blushing,

"I'm happy for you man," Stephanie said walking off. Dean walked over to me and noticed that I was starting to feel a little anxious about everything that was happening. It was probably the fact that my fate in this town was going to be revealed shortly and I didn't know what was bound to happen, and I didn't know if I was going to stay in this town or not with everyone. I was getting scared, but I didn't want to show it. Especially towards Dean.

"So...are you scared?" Dean asked me,

I nodded, I nodded softly and could feel my heart beating faster and faster, and I didn't want Dean to notice that I was getting more and more anxious by the second, and I was in public so I definitely didn't want to cry or freak out.

"Ev..." Dean said noticing me about to cry, "Are you alright?"

"I'm sorry, I'm just thinking too much." I sighed

"You have nothing to be sorry about Evelyn." Dean said, "Absolutely nothing, I get it, It's all overwhelming."

"I just want it all to be over with," I said,

"I know, and it will be."

CHAPTER THIRTY

Trixie

I looked around and watched as my sisters were talking to their friends. I saw Evelyn with Stephanie and Dean, and then Winnifred with Valerie and Jenny, I was really hoping that everything was going to go smoothly, but I also had a lot of what if's in my head, but that wasn't really a good thing. I felt someone tap my shoulder, and I turned around to see Max. He was smiling at me, and I didn't understand why, it was definitely no smiling matter.

"Hi stranger," Max said, "So how are you feeling,"

"A little nervous...actually super nervous." I said, "But a part of me actually wants to try and be optimistic, not only for me but for the girls."

"Well, you're doing a great job, and I don't doubt that you will going forward and I can't wait to see what you do next,"

"Thank you max. And I wish you the best of luck with Valerie."

Max laughed and he hugged me and I hugged him back, as we both let go, we both let out some laughter, hoping that everything was going to be okay. But with the way everything was we didn't know. But so far, I heard a lot of good things from our friends, but it was our friends. Of course they were going to say nice things about us in front of us.

I didn't know what was next, I didn't know if things were going to be okay. I looked over at Max and then took his hand. And then Winnie walked over to me for comfort.

"You okay Trixie?" She asked me

"I'm scared if I'm being honest." I answered laughing awkwardly. Winnie then grabbed my other hand and looked at me. I was just waiting for the final verdict and waiting to know where Winnie and Evelyn's fate was going to be. Whether it was here, or in a group home, but this was their home. They belonged in New York with everyone else, and they belonged with the rest of their friends and family that loved them, and how would they survive if they lived far away from them.

Because Winnifred would not be able to grow if she lived in a Girl's home, and Evelyn would never be able to get the life that she always wanted. And Dean was helping her grow and become a better woman and person, and especially in such a short amount of time. Dean also needed her as well, and was starting to really change because of her. They weren't done yet.

Dean walked over to me and asked to talk to me for a minute, of course, I agreed. Why did he want to talk to me? I didn't have a clue.

"So... I just wanted to tell you something, and this is something that I would never admit to anyone," Dean started, "But I really don't want Evelyn to leave, I don't want her out of my life I kind of want to keep her around..."

"I know you do," I said, "You haven't been that discreet about it."

"Yeah I know…" Dean said, "I'm trying to tell you, is when I said that I was falling in love with her…I meant it…I meant every single word."

"Did you really?" I asked him

Dean nodded.

I just looked at him for a minute and I hugged him tightly and almost saw tears coming out of my face. He was what she needed, and she was what he needed. And I was happy for both of them, and I had a feeling everything was going to turn out well for them, because opposites do attract, and I learned that from my parents.

I let go of Dean and I thanked him for everything he had done for me and for my sisters, and then he responded with a "You're Welcome" it seemed genuine which was something no one really expected from him, let alone myself, who I started off hating in the beginning of all of this. And then he ended up helping me and being my friend at the end of the day, I just wish I knew I could trust him earlier. Because then I wouldn't have been the hot headed girl I usually am and wouldn't have lost my temper on him, but that's what happens when I get protective of people, especially when it comes to my own sisters.

The Recess ended, and I watched as everyone go into the courtroom, I called for Winnie and Evelyn, calling for them to sit with me, and I wanted to grab both of their hands for the occasions. As I sat down in the middle of them, with Evelyn holding on hand and Winnie holding on to the other, I looked over at the both of them and sighed. Hearing what the judge had to say, this was it. Their fate was about to be revealed.

"I have heard from friends and family to the Martin Sisters, and I have come up with a decision," Judge said, "I have decided to place Winnifred Martin and her sister Evelyn Martin in the custody of their older sister Trixie."

Everyone was cheering and I cried tears of joy, I didn't think this was going to happen, I was scared we lost it once and for all. But we didn't. I got my girls back and I was getting everything I had ever wanted. I wasn't dreaming and I started pinching myself to see if I was dreaming, but I wasn't. I won. I won the court case, and I was going to raise my girls and be the best for them.

EPILOGUE
FOUR YEARS LATER

Winnifred

Life lately had seem to have gotten so much better for me. I had gotten into Columbia University for their Journalism Program, which is a dream of mine I have been holding onto for years. And if it weren't for my friends and family, I don't think I would have gotten as far as I did. And Boy I am relieved to be where I am. Of course, there is going to be loans in the process and I need a little bit of help financially but I can still do it. I think I can do it... scratch that I know I can do it and hopefully I'll be the first in my family to complete college, and hopefully, I can get my degree on time.

As for my friends, I haven't seen them in a while, after Valerie turned eighteen she moved to New Mexico to start a new life on her own. I do write to her from time to time, and it seems like she is doing alright, she just needed to find herself and figure out who she was on her own. And being on her own, I think she could definitely do that. She was always independent and if she stayed in the city where trouble was always brewing, she was never going to grow and all of us knew that about her. I do think about her constantly and I always hope that one day I do see her again, and she definitely will be a different person after everything. And I can't wait to see when she does grow as a person. She was always a good person, and a good friend, she just got caught in the wrong side of the tracks.

Jenny on the other hand was taken away from her parents a few months after my family court case and was sent to live with her Aunt in New Jersey, and the one to report her parents was Valerie's brother Max. I guess

Val told him and he said he was going to report it. I was happy that she was happy with her Aunt who was always Kind and Loving, I did visit her a little after my acceptance into Columbia and found out that she was in college to at the College of New Jersey and is studying History. I was so happy for her, I was happy to see that my best friend Jenny, who I didn't think was going to find her happy ending, finally find something that would make her happy. She does have moments where she has flashbacks of her parents and the awful things that they have done to her. But those flashbacks don't last forever. And I reminded Jenny constantly when I would go and see her. And I always hope for the best for her.

The day came when it was finally time for me to go to my first day at Columbia, I looked over at Trixie for support, who was open about how proud she was of me. I smiled at her and I smiled over at Evelyn.

Who gave me a hug, I could tell she was proud of me too.

I got to the campus. And it was a huge campus, especially since it was in the city. I couldn't believe my eyes, college was everything I had dreamed of and more. And I was going to make something of myself on my own, and there was so much that I had went through and I was going to move past it all. I knew that Mom and dad would be proud of how far I have come. I got inside the building and walked over to my first class and I found myself bumping into a Red-Headed tall girl.

"Sorry, I'm looking for the class intro to journalism," She said,

"That's where I'm going," I responded, "I'm Winnie."

"Nice to meet you, I'm Ruby."

"Are you a Journalism student?" I asked Ruby

"Yeah I am." Ruby said to me as the two of us wandered around looking for the classroom, after five minutes of wandering, we had finally found it. And we both sat down, and I saw a familiar face, it was Scarlett from the juvenile center.

"Winnifred. Winnifred Martin is that you?" Scarlett asked me

"Yes. It's me, how are you?"

"I'm alright," She responded, "How have you been?"

"I'm alright, and look at you... college student." I said excited, "I'm so happy that you got your life back on track."

"Me too, after I got released I sort of became a completely different person."

"I'm proud of you Scarlett..." I said, "You deserve it, you really deserve it."

I had a new chapter in my life, and I was moving on from everything. Everything that I had to conquer had got me to this particular moment, and it was worth it, all of it was completely and utterly worth it.

Evelyn

Dean and I were still going strong, we had been together for almost four years. And he has seen me at my highest and my lowest. And he never gave up on me, not one. And I don't know where I would be without him, I'd probably be somewhere where I wasn't happy.

Dean just made me happy in every way known to mankind, he saved me from the worst relationship of my life, and I had known for a while that I was going to marry Dean. Evelyn Richards had a nice ring to it, without a doubt.

And Dean got a job, a good job to potentially get a one-room apartment for me and him, and we moved in together a few months after Winnie started college. I watched as Trixie was watching her sisters grow up and move on with our lives, she was getting emotional just thinking about it. And she was happy seeing Dean grow into a completely different person, and he even said it was because of me, because he still would be a juvenile if I didn't exist, these were his words not mine.

As we got to our apartment, I couldn't help but look around at the place as the movers continued to put some stuff into the apartment, I watched and Dean wrapped his arms around my waist and I couldn't but laugh with him knowing how ticklish I was.

"You happy?" Dean asked me,

"Yeah I am," I said, "I really am, happier than ever."

"I'm glad, I'm glad I could do that," Dean said as he kissed my cheek, and went in for his lips. I just knew that Dean and I were going to have the best life together.

Weeks later, after finally settling in, Dean and I spent a lot of time in the apartment, talking about what was going to be next for our future. We both had a lot in the mind about what we were going to do, and there was so much we both wanted. We had ten or twenty years planned, of what was going to happen with us in the future. I didn't really think about much. I just wanted Dean in my life forever and I was hoping Dean felt the same way.

"Are you happy with me?" Dean asked me one day as we were both sitting on the couch,

"Of course I am, I wouldn't be living with you if I wasn't." I responded to him,

"Good..." Dean started to say, but then he sighed, thinking and I could tell he had something on his mind that he wanted to say, "Ummmm...Ev..."

"Yes?"

"Do you imagine a life with me?" He asked me,

"Of course I do." I responded and kissed his lips knowing that he needed that reassurance.

"So, will you do something for me?"

"What?"

Dean sighed, I deep down knew what he was going to ask. But I didn't want to spoil the moment for him and for myself.

"Will you marry me?" Dean asked, I didn't even answer I just kissed his lips passionately, he and I both took that as a Yes.

Trixie

I had spent the past four years figuring out my life, after Evelyn turned eighteen, I finished my final year of college and I am now working as a nurse officially, I have finally gotten the job that I had always wanted.

On top of that, I ended up raising a kid of my own, with Max. We had a boy named Gregory, Greg for short, named him after my father and He reminds me so much of my father, his eyes, his hair, his mannerisms, all of it and I missed my dad so much, and I promised myself I would tell little baby Greg all about his grandpa and how much he had done to make me the woman I was today.

Max and I had been married now for almost two years, and we had never been happier. He and I worked together and that is what made us work, and I didn't realize how well he and I worked until the baby was born, and boy we worked together as a good team. Max didn't remember the last time he saw Valerie and was hoping that one day she would meet baby Greg and she would have such an amazing bond with him. No matter how much Val hated kids, we both thought that she would definitely grow to like this kid in particular. In some ways, he had a little bit of snarky sass, just like his Aunt Valerie and Valerie would have loved to see all of that sass from a little baby and she would be proud too and I wouldn't be surprised if she ever taught my three year old son swear words.

“Do you ever think of her?” I asked Max as we were playing with little Greg.

“Yeah, all the time.” Max said, “Wherever she is, I hope nothing but the best for her.”

“She’ll come around, she’s stubborn but she’ll come back.” I added, I heard the doorbell ring and I didn't think much of it, Max said he would get the door and as he opened it, he almost started sobbing, I looked over and I didn't know why. I never seen Max cry before so it must be a good reason to cry. But then Max came by to me and Little Greg and I asked what it was and then I saw what it was, it was Valerie. I ran up to her and hugged her, and I couldn’t believe my eyes and let alone believe that she was here.

“What are you doing here?” I asked her

“I wanted to meet my nephew.” Valerie said, “Is that so much of a crime? Shit…”

“Shit…” We all heard baby Gregory say and I turned around and laughed and smacked Valerie on the arm.

“He’s going to learn those words one way or another.” Valerie said lifting up Baby Greg… “Hi, I’m your Aunt Valerie, and I am definitely going to be your favorite.”

“Hold it. Hold it.” I said walking over to her, “I thought you hated kids.”

“I do…” Val said staring at me and I could tell she was lying, “They poop, they cry and always have to have everything their way.”

I knew she was lying. She definitely wanted to be in my son’s life. And she wanted to grow to love her nephew.

“How long are you planning on staying?” Max asked her, “Are you planning on going back to New Mexico anytime soon?”

“Actually I was thinking about staying for good.” Val said looking at me and Max, “If that’s okay.”

“Of course it’s okay.” I said hugging Val, she was definitely like another sister to me, and I loved her like one as well.

“I have a place, I got a small little apartment, on my own, I made enough money and I was able to get my act together a bit in New Mexico, but there was a part of me that really missed all of you.” Valerie said to me and Max and then she kissed Baby Greg on the forehead.

“I just have to know one thing.” Max started to say, “Who are you and what have you done to Valerie?”

Both of us chuckled, and looked over to see Winnifred returning from school, Valerie walked over to her and hugged her, I had never seen Winnifred more excited to see her best friend that she hadn't seen in two years. It felt great for both me and Max to see our sisters in the same roof again. Minutes later I heard the phone ring, and I picked it up.

"Hello?" I said,

"Trix, it's Evelyn." Evelyn said on the phone, "I gotta tell you something but you can't freak out, actually you can,"

"What is it?"

"Dean and I are engaged." She blurted out of excitement.

"What?" I covered my mouth out of excitement, and turned over to everyone else, "Guys, Evelyn and Dean are engaged."

Winnifred started cheering out of excitement.

"I'm so happy for those kids." Valerie drawled and clapped,

"Do you two want to come over for dinner to celebrate?" I asked her,

"Sure I would love to." She said,

"How about 6:30?"

"I agree, we'll be there." Evelyn said and I hung up, I couldn't help but start crying. Only because all of this was going so well for all of us. Winnifred was starting college, Evelyn is getting married and now I had a son of my own, all of us were doing well and moving on with our lives, there were so much that we were doing and we were all going to be happy, after everything all of us went through we all deserved it.

I couldn't wait to see what was going to happen now, and then forever and as long as both of my sisters were in my life, I knew that everything was going to work out the way it should, and everything was going to matter as long as I had my family.

Made in the USA
Middletown, DE
30 September 2023

39846549R00215